Head in the Clouds,
Feet Treading Water

Navigating the Human Condition

Mark McCallister

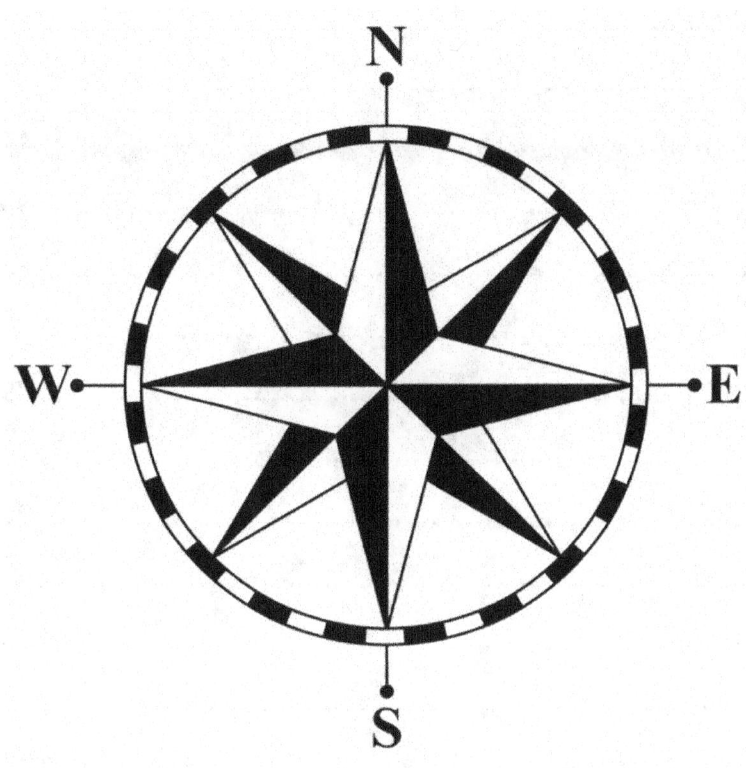
N
W
E
S

Contents

The Longest Journey

When you see the lights of Nirvana, you'll always find home.
All hearts are true, and born alone.
Give back what you take, no charity lost.
Not far from the tree, and all for not.
Don't forget yourself, for you must keep
Not all is lost, What is sowed is reaped.
For time will tell, and all is well,
From Wence it came, and ones own Hell.
A deathly kiss, to seal the deal,
Believe or not, for thou must feel.
All is new, and that True blue,
All pain is kept, thou honor Too,
For Strength to feed, everyone must bleed.
Words on the page for all to read.
We come and go, all Eb and Flow,
Must follow through, ones Spirit knows.
While your still here, No Death, No Fear.
When once is done, a Final tear.
A waterfall, and that's not all,
The soul that's kept, is never small.
Don't beg or plead, For spirits read,
Back to the Start, A planted seed.
At ones Last Breath, a Peaceful Death,
Time ticks away, so one can rest.
A cross must bear, Forgiveness shared,
For Heavens Hope, A net is Snared.
First things first, for things to grow,
All Love will come, please take it Slow.
Whatever possible, Love conquers all,
Everyone must board, No Ships to Small.
To give no more, Till All Ashore.
 All come Home, Through Heavens Door.

-Mark McCallister

"When the student is ready, the teacher will appear."

-The Buddha

Introduction

"If the people who rule you tell you the kingdom is in the sky, the birds will get there first, if they tell you it is in the sea, the fish will get there first, rather the kingdom is inside you, and all around you. Lift a stone and you will find me. Split a piece of wood, and I am there."

-Jesus Christ

The human experience

In this text I will discuss the human condition, explaining that in life, there is a path to the sublime, and our very existence is on an inexorable path to the achievable. Enlightenment is a state of mind, and spirituality is found in following one's own path. There is a remarkable kinship among all beings in this search for truth. In our shared human condition, our search is for more than mere life; it is a quest for the attainable. I will explain how all things are aligned, that myriad details are all components of a greater plan. That mere survival is an insignificant portion of the challenge of being human, and that during our brief existence we are all part of a shared humanity, a shared human condition which must be understood. There is a sense to existence, a pattern - like the wheel of Dharma. We are all traversing similar life-paths, yet in distinct ways. Life is life, and we simply must live it. Understanding our human condition is the key.

Path to the achievable

The path to the achievable is real, and our mortality is intended to make us seek something greater. The path towards that 'something greater' is already set; we are compelled to pursue it, and that pursuit requires navigation tools. All things are aligned, pointing us towards a greater design. Merely living our lives is insufficient; we must find our own personal "True North." Once we discover this, then navigating according to our spiritual and moral compass is all that is required.

 Overcoming what we face is the key to a higher existence. If Utopia is your goal, then Earth is a good start to finding it. There are many philosophies on attaining a greater reality. However, one must discover the truth for themselves. The path to the achievable is the one true quest of all mankind. We are looking for something greater than existence. So, if you are looking for something larger than life, continue reading and we will discover it together.

Great minds think alike

There have been many people who have tried to teach us how to find the path. Many books have tried to provide instruction. In this text I will discuss the many complicities and shared simplicities of these teachings. These teachings have spanned for thousands of years. Throughout time there have been tutors for a more spiritual life. There have been great teachers since the beginning of time. But where have they gone. From the I Ching, and the Tao, to the Tibetan Book of the Dead, and the Bible. So many great teachings from the past seemingly forgotten. So many teachers; their messages, lost to time. But where does that leave us. Where do we stand. Understanding that the "Basic Instructions Before Leaving Earth," is merely a jumping off point. Is it possible that we ourselves can transcend existence? The great teachers of the past spent their lives searching for the answer to this. And as hidden as this answer is, may it one day be rediscovered. Understanding that there is something greater to contemplate, maybe something you might want to hear. Something that can be taught, but we must be courageous enough to get up and challenge ourselves to look, listen, and learn. Only then will you understand. There is nothing greater than passing on the knowledge to enlighten those around you. Where have all the great teachers gone? Who is the next one to arise? Has history forgotten the lessons of the soul? The Buddha, the Christ, and all the others who chose the path before them as an eternal measure to an end that is indescribable. In fact, their teachings have not been lost to time. Their teachings are everywhere. Great men have tried, but if you don't look at it with a clear vision you cannot see what the message is. It has been the quest of all mankind, since the beginning of time. You are not the first person to question their existence. We all want life to be ours to control. But are you willing to accept the fact that there is perhaps a greater understanding of the truth. To feel comfortable with something larger than yourself. For it is within us and all around us. The truth is as Jesus would say, "Lift a stone and I am there, split a piece of wood and you will find me." Do not get me wrong, I am of no denomination, but of am one Earth, one presence. Perhaps finding yourself is easier than you think. There have been many teachers, those who have tried to make us understand the truth - that there is more to life than what may seem. From the Bible to Buddhism; from the Koran, to the Bhag avid Ghita, and the Tao. Are you willing to search for the many ways to find the path? Do you have the courage and strength to see the world for what it is? Many have followed, only to find the truth. And those that have found the path, understand what it means to be human. If the student is selfless then the lesson is learned. When the lesson is learned, one may become the teacher. When one teaches, more will understand. To grow like a plant is the idea. But first you must understand the seed of existence. This seed, that has been planted repeatedly throughout time. This seed is something you must plant for yourself. Only then will you be able to grow, and bear fruit of your own. Fruit that must be shared, so that others may plant seeds of their own. In this pattern we can succeed in a search for a greater reality. So let us plant the seed together. So that together we may grow.

Understanding is the key

There is a path laid before us. There is so much out there to learn. But this is only the beginning. It can only come from within. Understanding that enlightenment, or even that the achievable is within reach. Because the truth is in you. There have been so many religions on this home we call Earth. So many philosophies and ideas. And all have been about overcoming your mortal existence to achieve something greater. That there is something better out there, and that if you would only quiet yourself long enough to seek, you can find. There are no boundaries before you in your search for something more. Other than the history of mankind, the ones who came before us, and the truth that they tried to introduce to us. Some look at this existence as an excuse to do what they want. But there are those that look further. It should not bother you that there is more to this life than mere existence. That there is a greater idea to all of this, and that it should not make you feel unincluded or unimportant. We want so much to define ourselves as something different that we miss the bigger picture that we all are involved in this greater reality. Is it so bad that there is a path set before your feet and that we are all part of something greater?

First, we must understand that we are all here to learn. This is found in our daily lives; in the measures we take to become enormously greater than what we appear to be. We must accept the idea that there is more out there.

Lead by example, but how can one lead until they understand how to follow. When you have learned something should it not to be said that you should understand fully. And if you understand fully, it should not be said that you shouldn't teach it. "Teach a man to fish," they say. Well, that is exactly the point. Let's fish together for some time. Let us see what we can catch…what we can understand. Perhaps we can bring up our awareness of something greater than what we already know. Let us set out on a quest to discover together. Perhaps we shall discover this path, locate our compass, and navigate to our own "True North." Only then will you be able to see the larger picture. Only then will you see the truth.

The Basics

Most people are not ready to understand. They are afraid. Those who are afraid are only discouraged by what they feel. Those that feel are only cheated by their own vices. Those that understand their own foolishness can only be encouraged by their own virtue. Those that have found virtue, stand in the threshold of the doorway to a greater reality. Realizing that there is a better road to take is a good start. Tomorrow is another day and there is always a chance to live a better life. All you must do is wake up and challenge yourself. Every day, you can transform into something better. Life can be chaotic. One would think that an obedience to an order will solve this problem. It does not. Obedience only will shut you down. Instead, embrace these difficulties, and make your own decisions. So many misconceptions of a life worth living are portrayed through a manner of conformity. I say, escape all of this. The only way to live life is head on. Weather the storm. Find a sense of awareness that fits with your soul's purpose.

A way that you can feel comfortable with an existence beyond what you have already experienced. And to start at the root would be first to understand how to grow. Every blossom of your life should reflect how you want to live, and every petal is a step in the right direction in how much more you want to become. We are all dying... but to remember that we are also so very alive. From a life lived to an existence which we would so like to be a part of. We must embrace the certainty of death as a jumping off point to living a life we want to live. The Samurai would call this Bushido. Life in every breath.

The Simple Truth

The idea is simple, that there is a pattern to everything under the sun. And that if a better life is the goal; then these simple truths would simply be a connect the dots experience for you. All I can do is show you the way, you must be the one to walk it. To exist and coexist amongst others is the goal of all mankind. Granted, we all are on the same path in this life. We are all merely doing the same thing in different ways, and at different times. But the experience and the message are the same. Although I cannot tell you what to do. I can tell you how to do it. It all ends the same. Death is certain, life is not. The question is, would you be willing to do whatever it takes to live a higher existence? To follow the path is to find, "True North." To navigate it is to experience the human condition. The spiritual and moral compass exists to help you guide yourself along the road. To find that the idea of the achievable is found right here on Earth. The Earth is the place where you find your way. To admit that we all live in our own Hell is also true. To want to rise above all of it is the true path to greatness. Don't ever settle for less. You are worth every bit of this existence. Regardless of religion or philosophy. You are worth every spiritual penny spent, as an investment in a future kingdom that no one can quite understand. As a matter of fact, each and every one of you will learn how to use your compass as a means to this greater reality. It is up to us to recognize our place, where we are, where we're going, and where we want to be.

When I say we all know who and where we are; I mean that all of us can feel in our heart and soul exactly what holds us back and what pushes us forward. That we know truly where we stand. It is a question that can be answered simply. We all know what we need to do to rise above. All we must do is find it in our mind, our hearts and our souls to understand how important that is to us. We are all stuck on the same path. One must just learn how to navigate it. This is where the compass comes in.

The pattern is simple. It begins with our basic instinct to fear. For fears are the most primitive thoughts that we have. It is followed only by emotions, which are the most basic values we possess. This precedes the idea of vice, followed by virtue. These can all be understood as equally important and pieces to living one's everyday life. Only we as humans can decide right and wrong. We also must fall to get back up. So, in essence, we can only learn to do right by first doing wrong. I will describe how all of this plays out as an equally important role in understanding one's ability to process life as it comes at you. Once understood, it is easy to manifest these values in your daily lives and improve your everyday reality based on your ability to navigate through these obstacles. Once understood fully, your everyday life becomes a constant stream of upholding positive values over negative ones. Ultimately making your life an easier stream of conscious ideas and values.

Simply put, there is an animalistic value to life as well as a human one. The animal part is found in instincts and fears. These are primitive basic functions to life. What sets us apart from animals is our ability to constructively formulate these functions into a higher conscious. Thereby separating us from other animals. But to understand what we are we must first understand where we come from. So, in order to understand the basis of humanity we must first contemplate our origins. When all is understood you will know what it means to live freely and be able to consciously make decisions based solely on one's ability to process these fundamental aspects of everyday life. This sets you apart from other forms of life and puts you on your path to the human conception of the achievable. Experiencing the human condition is your starting point. All humanity begins and ends here. It is not about who is faster or slower. One's success will come from how well you experience the journey. Slow is smooth, and smooth is fast.

~ 18 ~

Humans have always searched for something greater than us. I say we must search ourselves to find something greater. Is greatness achievable? Does meditation and prayer bring us closer to it? Is enlightenment attainable? Perhaps this is all true. But it is up to us to discover it for ourselves. The truth must be experienced. We all have an equal opportunity to find our own way to something greater. But how do we find it. Is there a map, a compass, a road to it? I say there is. And once understood, all one needs to do is simply live it. Once one understands how to live it, it simply becomes "The way." There is a universal order to all things. You merely must peer into the void and discern the truth for yourself. Who knows what will gaze back. Many have searched for the truth, many have found it, and many have taught it. Once found it is the most empowering knowledge you will ever know. To look behind the curtain and find the truth. It will forever change your life. You will begin to see it manifest in your everyday life. A tool to piloting your existence is the goal to becoming something more than just ordinary. To ascend the mere everyday life and setting you upon a path to the attainable, is the idea. These secrets have been kept for thousands of years. In hopes that one day, they will be discovered again and understood. We all begin and end, but to find our own way to something greater is the common goal. There are many routes to take to find it, but it is all the same game. We must play the field. Only then will we understand life. Only then will we know the truth. The truth is, "YES!" We can become something larger than life. This does not make you better than anyone, only better than the self you want to empower. Once this path is walked it is forever known. It is learnable, it is teachable. It is not selfish to want to be better. Once you understand you will be humbled by the truth. Acquiring knowledge is an unselfish means to learning the truth.

~ 20 ~

Something we can share, something we can pass on. Knowledge and wisdom have been the focus of mankind for a very long time. This search seems to have been forgotten these days. People want everything done for them. They don't want to do the work for themselves. Yet the truth is, is that the only one that can uncover these ideas, is you. It is not something you can buy; it is not something you can sell. It is only learnable and teachable. And once set upon the path it is inescapable.

What I Hope You Will Learn

So, in this text I will try to encourage you to think outside the box. Reach your own conclusions. Take what you want and leave the rest behind. There is a cosmic design that is fractal. This pattern is called life. Much like the Buddhist idea of Dharma. And who would you be to not want to learn how to live it better. In this text I will explain the simplicity of a life that can only be obtained through understanding. That there is a life worth living. That the rewards must be shared. And what better than an existence to share with all the ones who walk the face of the Earth. All those that you share it with, will create their own path to the achievable. I believe in all forms of spirituality. That all the paths are the same and to the same end. Whether or not you read the rest of this book and obtain these lessons is up to you.

Nirvana, Heaven, Hell, Limbo, Earth; these are all states of being. The question is how you want to live or should I say, survive these realms of existence. To know the path is eternally in your favor, when you choose to accept the same journey as everyone else who is on the road. Not to look at your voyage here as the same selfishly gratifying method as you have become accustomed to. Rather to accept that we are all here to find the same destination. To think that you are here merely for your own existence can fool you. That you are above all else is insane. Although to accept the fact that we are all here on the same experience, is the path to the achievable. Eventually all paths lead into one. Choosing how fast and far you go is up to you. How you want to spend your time here is up to you. Can I tell you one path is better than all the rest? NO! But I can at least let you know that there is more to life than meets the eye.

That we are all part of one greater existence. Whether or not you accept this is up to you. But who would I be to teach you anymore that you are willing to learn. The beauty of all life is the understanding that there is something better. Understanding that there is more is the key. The idea that you can become it is the path to the achievable. So, in this doctrine I will do my best to explain my thoughts on the matter. Hopefully by the end of it you will also have concluded that whatever it means to be a human in a greater sense, is something you look forward to discovering. That all that read this book, will hopefully understand what thousands of years of held back philosophies will hold for your search for your own reality. These are teachings passed down through the ages hidden and obscured so that no one would know the truth. And with good reason, for are you truly worthy of knowing the truth.

I will describe in this doctrine all the truths as I have found manifest and which we so strongly believe to be authentic. And through that truth I hope you will find some clear message that clicks for you. So, recollect on these teachings and answer for yourself, "Was it worth it?" There is a pattern to life. It is all the same as much as it is different. As soon as you understand these and their similarities you will fully understand the pattern to life and its fundamental value. That there is a method to the madness and once understood, life can be a simple progression of easy decisions. To know that we all share in this thing called life and that we all have the same ability to rise above and triumph over everyday existence. It is up to you to decide that life is more than just yourself. Once this is understood, the world is yours.

I am here only to show you the path, give you the map, and the compass. How far you want to go with it is up to you. I am not here to fool you. Excellence is found within. It does not make you better than anyone. Although I would say it does make you responsible for your own fate. There is no way to pretend to be ignorant once the knowledge is within you. And it will make it impossible to forget the truth. If this sounds fascinating, read further. I will do my best to illuminate you on the truth and its benefits to your everyday life. So please read further and I hope I can be of aid in enlightening your way on the road to truth and happiness. The way to "True North."

Fear

"The only thing to fear is fear itself"

-Friedrich Wilhelm Nietzsche

So, you have read this far, perhaps we can further explore the model that we call the human condition. Like all animals, our thoughts in their most primitive form come as instincts or, furthermore, what is perhaps best described as fear. Yes, fear, the most basic of all thought processes. It is a static condition unless confronted, it can consume. Fear is the mind-killer. Like cancer in us, it spreads from place to place, infecting us with its unwanted presence. The concept of instinct is a direct reaction to this fear. The question is, is there some concept or design to these fears?

Is there a blueprint for how they come about. Can they be dealt with? Can they be overcome? I am here to tell you, "Yes!" they can be. Like everything, they form a pattern, like a design on a rug, strewn piece by piece to make a whole. There is a pathway, of course, through fear. Through the swamp of despair. To far greener land than we have ever seen. So many try to escape from their fears by running away, to no avail. Fear is not conquered through ignorance. The only real method through madness is simply applying knowledge, finding awareness, and dealing with one's everyday life through these simple understandings. That there is an outline to everything, and like a pattern, something that can be navigated like a map. Or, more importantly...a compass. On this spiritual and moral compass, I shall help you on your path to insight. With this compass, you shall navigate the depths of the human soul and realize humankind's design. As a prism, you can examine and see the intrinsic values that we call our everyday lives. Once understood, you will never be the same. There are no two ways about it. Either you know and understand this pattern and can set yourself on a course to personal growth and happiness, or blindly walk through life. Losing yourself at every which way to the misunderstanding of one's state of mind. This is not a selfish means to an end, but a path to insight. You may uncover the simple realities about your own existence and everyone else's lives as well.

Understanding how to navigate the compass is the focus. And the beginning of this compass is to set yourself upon the path to, "True North." "True North," would be the understanding that all we do in life has a direction. And the clearest insight into this relationship of oneself is fear. Like an animal in the wild, our instincts guide us. So why would we, as humans, think that we deviate so much from this necessary fundamental reaction to stimuli? Although humans can reason far beyond most animals, we still have the basic instinct to overcome the fears that make their way into our lives.

Our entire social identity is based on overcoming fears to fit in with the masses. To not stand out, in fear of rejection. To blend with our surroundings in hopes of not being found to be different. "The opiate for the masses," so to speak, is wanting to fit in. But what if I told you that most people who want to test your ability to deal with fear, only want to make an example of you. What if I told you they do not know how to navigate the minefield of fear. That they want to see your reaction to it in a social experiment called, "Survival of the fittest." If you could only find the means to navigate this hazard on your own and save the wisdom for yourself, rather than serve as a social experiment for others. Then one could help others find the same. A way to pilot this representation of life. A means to the end that we who have navigated it call it, "True North." Once your compass is set, you will be well on your way to the truth. That enlightenment and the path to the achievable is not found in a book, it is located within you. That the teachings of great masters, have not been forgotten, and are still applied in our lives today. To decipher the riddle of life. This all begins with the understanding that the most basic of all thoughts is ...fear. To overcome fear, one must know what fear is. It's a simple idea, really. It is one's reaction to stimuli, at its most essential level. And in this text, I will describe that even fear can be found to have a pattern. A construct, a way through the labyrinth. A path to where one can walk through fear. Of course, first you must admit that you are afraid. Do not be so lost in social life that you deny yourself the most fundamental value, the most elementary idea. That we humans are no more than evolved mammals. The only difference is the ability to reason in a means that is greater than all other animals. But if I told you that the most basic of animal natures, leads to understanding the truth... would you listen? If I said to you that understanding how to deal with fear as an animal would help you navigate your spiritual compass as a human...would you take note? The problem is that over the ages, the social construct, or matrix, has become such a paradigm of existence that we have lost ourselves to its complexities. One must understand at the basic level the difference between surviving socially and leading the way, is to overcome. By overcoming, I mean, to defeat fear. Although the matrix has become so bent that many believe that overcoming is impossible. Overcoming is found in one's ability to deal with life as it comes. To be independent of others in one's abilities to navigate upon this map we call existence.

Understanding the plan and knowing how to read your compass is all you need to know to navigate your everyday life. And all of this begins with understanding fear. Where does it come from, where does it lead us, where does it end. Well, I will tell you, it never ends. But our ability to deal with it always improves as we deal with its effects. I also have to say that it leads us to our purpose. And that there are basic fears that are always constant. That there is a design to it. And that your soul will thank you for acquiring the knowledge to overcome these fears. Like a kaleidoscope or prism, there is a pattern to everything. I will explain how these fears fit into this pattern and how everything is aligned. So that we can move further into the consciousness of the soul. Life has a design, and it is simple. Understanding the basis of this model should be one's goal in life. To living a more fulfilling existence. Understanding the spiritual realm is practically necessary to overcome anything more than a merely unaware social life. Although fitting in and living socially is an easy means to what one might think is happiness. It will not prove itself to be of benefit in the long run. Happiness is a choice. One can walk the path to enlightenment. One may walk the path of least resistance. One way leads to a full life. One will leave your spiritual cup empty. It is only a matter of time before one discovers this. In this text, I will describe how to eliminate the emptiness and provide a spiritually full cup, something which is often overlooked, something that has been misinterpreted through the ages. Also, something that is there just beyond our reach. Something behind the shade. Perhaps something overlooked. So, sit back, relax, and enjoy this book. I assure you that after reading it, you will find the resources to fill your cup and live a fruitful life.

Want

We will begin with the most basic of fears... to want. I know you may be confused. How could want of anything be a fear? To want is bitter-sweet, people search for getting what they want their whole lives. Sometimes we get it. Sometimes we don't. Not getting what one wants can cause one to fear wanting again. Getting what one wants can will make you want more. So essentially, to want can be fearful. We spend our whole lives doing it. It is merely a roadblock. Something that discourages us from ever getting what we truly deserve. It's a disguise to avoid the truth. Something misleading. It is motionless, untiring, continuously there to impede your path to happiness. For real pleasure does not rely merely on getting what you want. To receive something can be wonderful. However, being grateful for what we get is the most important lesson here.

Too much want can be perplexing. Getting what we want can lead to self-destruction.

Moderation here is the key. Although how does one sensibly want. A goal is one thing, and to achieve it is genuinely an accomplishment. However, to consistently want can be destructive. As it is said, "To want is to err, and to err is divine." But at one point, one must grow up and put aside these wants. When we are young, to want seems sensible. We are only testing ourselves, trying to find a way through the madness of getting older. At one point, we must look deep within ourselves and realize that when we want, we put aside ourselves and begin to assimilate into the social construct. Trying to find ourselves in the world can be dangerous. We want so badly to fit in that we lose our base. Our spiritual base must become a collective bedrock. Those that see your weaknesses will exploit them at every turn for their own benefit. Others can see this want in you. They can tangle you in a web that only destroys your real identity. The question is, "Would you sacrifice your self-worth, to fit in?" The world has found itself on the idea that, "Only the strong survive." So how can you survive if you are not strong enough to see things for yourself. You do not need others to find happiness, only a strong self-worth. Let those around you cling to you for wisdom, rather than you adhere to an inconspicuous value that others may give you.

Is it up to others to define you? I say, "No!" I say it is up to you to determine who you are. And to consistently want can only destroy you. Achievement can be a blessing, but too much gain can be harmful. To obtain without any effort is only fooling yourself into thinking that receiving is easy. Everyone is chasing after something. If you merely want what everyone else has, then continue on that path. If you're going to find the truth, realize how you want to be seen. Would you instead fit in and be like everyone else? Or become a beacon of individualism, for all to see. To have others depend upon you for guidance. To be the student that becomes the teacher. We grow up in the social construct to believe that to fit in is our best chance at survival. Will others remember you as a follower, or as someone who will take the lead. Unfortunately, most will cast you down for being different. In the eyes of others to not belong is somehow a weakness. They might say, "To belong is the only path to true happiness." I would say that this all is the wool that has been pulled over your eyes. The fog in a steam-soaked mirror that can only mask the truth before you. If wanting what everyone else has in mind is your goal, then acquiring truth is beyond your comprehension. However, to want what is least seen and is perhaps more significant. The path of, "True North," can be your saving grace. To know who you are beyond this basic social model is to search the ever-illusive truth. That we are all here to grow and become better human beings.

I believe that it is vital to know who you are. However, we are often thrown into life without all the understanding that it takes to lead such a lifestyle. If left unchecked, one will only submit to the will of the masses. However, we are always baffled by the idea of want. We all do it. We all live it.

Moreover, we all crave to wanting. Left unchecked, one will lose himself in the shadow of greed. This understanding will come later in this text. So, all we must consider is, "what do we really want?" Getting what you want is also a part of this social model. This is all to mislead you into thinking that what you want is what others have. It's a power game, and no one will let you get the better of them. So, you must try to get the better of yourself. Understand that mere wanting is a daydream. Acquiring what you wish is elusive. And the idea of going on wanting is an absurdity. "Once bitten twice shy." Shall you push harder to lead, to find the truth? Or will you give in to the matrix, the social construct that is there to blind you from the actual reality?

Many are not ready to be awakened to the truth. But for those that are looking, perhaps you will find your answers here. We search our whole lives for an existence that is ours. Is it easier to give in, or to stand up? To realize that wanting is only the beginning. Looking beyond that pale veil of uncertainty is what we were looking for all along. To continually challenge ourselves to search for the truth, is in fact, the only truth. That we don't exactly fit in with the social theory of belonging.

That we must separate ourselves from the masses to discover this truth.

It is ok to question what is going on in our lives. At an early age, it is ok to not understand. It is ok to want to belong. But by a certain point, we must question what our goals really are. Are we leaders, or are we followers? Do we continue through life forever, wanting? Or is the fear to want enough to understand that we do not always get what we are looking for. That want is merely another means of control over our true selves. Something to keep us in line with the rest of society. To blind us from the truth that we are all here on an independent mission for the truth. If knowledge is the only truth then the only power is to understand this awareness, this personal explanation of our existence. This ever-elusive truth that seems to escape us all. That truthfully, we are all alone in our journey to the path to happiness. It is something that can be taught, it is something that can be learned. But in all openness, it can only be achieved through personal exploration: personal conquest, the triumph of self, a delicate balance of discovery.

We cannot escape wanting. We can only control how we want and what we want for. To be like everyone else is a false journey. To find oneself is the only real actuality. To want for self is selfish. To want for personal gain is equally as damaging. To search for self-enlightenment is an unselfish act, one that can only better you. It can only bring us closer to the truth. That only through a search for personal character, can one find their identity. Many have tried to teach this through the ages. Being taught is a gift. To not obscure the teachings of wisdom will lead to actual personal gain.

Real personal growth comes from within. So, it is there that we start our search. To look within, deep within. To whom we indeed are. To what we want to become. No more is required for self-realization. Only the focus on being oneself can overcome the want to being what everyone else wants you to be. To rise above and pursue an identity that will lead you to the balance of truth. Rather than mislead us into thinking that we are only as good as everyone else will allow you to become... the sense of self.

To be truthful, to want is not evil. But it can be a roadblock in our path to self-enlightenment. This enlightenment is so crucial to our growth as individuals and human beings. It is ok to want, but what to want for. Is it a personal goal or is it a means to an end that will always escape you. Is it for personal growth, or for public review? Can one judge the importance of want? Is it something that can be lectured? How do we navigate ourselves to the truth? Is it ok to fear what we want or to welcome want as a challenge to overcome? I would have to say it is a fear to comprehend. Something to welcome. A journey and a passage to a better life. In essence, to want is only a barrier to personal enlightenment—something to conquer. Triumph over the fear of want is the first step into a larger world, a more abundant life.

This is the beginning of a journey beyond your imagination. Overcoming the fear of want is the basis for all other accomplishments—the first step upon the path. The system is simple, and once you learn how to navigate it, how much easier your life will become. The primary fear of want is the steppingstone to higher learning—the first degree upon the spiritual compass in which, "True North" can be found.

The only thing that can mislead you is wanting itself. You will wish to have what others have; they will want what you have. To figure out what is just want and what is genuinely obtainable, is found within. This search is constant. Forever continuing in our everyday lives.

You must always be pursuing a higher path. As each piece is discovered and rediscovered, the easier the journey is. So, I must ask you to stay constant. Once learned, the way will lead you; all you must do is have the courage to walk along the path. I guarantee you if others knew what you know, they would follow. And once your successes become an example, the ones that follow will have nothing more than respect for your wisdom. Wisdom is the goal of every day, that there is a way to continually learn, grow, and become something greater than our own imagining. Others will only be able to look upon in admiration for your quest for knowledge. To save yourself and others from social theory. That we are all aimlessly wandering around with only our wants to guide us. Instead of discovering the truth, that what we want is only there to mislead you. What is more significant than personal triumph. And what is more abundant than overcoming the social experiment. To stay calm in the tornado of wants is to discover what is of real importance. All you must do is decide whether you want to be like everyone else or set yourself upon the path to individuality. Once upon this journey, you will never escape the truth. You will forever be in the process of exploration. The only destination upon this path will be your experience on the road to personal enlightenment. A continuation of your individual achievement as a human being. With this knowledge you acquire you will forever be more grateful than to merely just wander upon a life that has no clear path. To realize being human is the truth, and your spiritual compass will guide you. So, sit back and relax, the journey is about to begin.

The more you learn, the more you become whole. To understand that we are all here upon the same path is the only real determining factor for oneself. To not lose hope that there is something more significant. That all we must do is set ourselves in the right direction. The direction of, "True North." And let our everyday lives be a search upon this compass to a more fruitful existence.

Loss

The next hurdle to achieving personal enlightenment is in understanding the fear of loss. No one wants to lose. It's hard to even imagine losing. We all have special things in our lives that we want to keep, to treasure. One can only understand what it is to lose by recognizing what we have. This is tricky, because how can we value what we have, without the fear of losing what is essential to us. One can only wish that we have what we have forever. However, the reality is much more hard to bear than the mere thought of losing. To experience loss, one must have to lose. This is a growing period for us as humans. It makes us grateful for what we still have. It is a gift to enjoy the time we have with what we stand to lose. The truth is all loss is the same, the more we want, the more we have, the more we stand to lose. This can lead someone to think that they shouldn't have anything. To find the beauty in what we have is the right path to understanding loss. The greater the possession, the greater the feeling of sorrow when we lose it. This can steer some away from valuing what we have. The more we have, the more we stand to lose…always. To find the value in what we have is the goal of understanding the fear of loss. To lose is an inevitable fact that cannot be escaped.

So, we can fool ourselves into thinking what we have is not that big of a deal and miss the point entirely. But to realize that our cup is filled one day and is empty the next, is the truth. Do not fool yourself into thinking you get to keep all that you possess. The beauty in life is to recognize what we have and to enjoy it while it lasts. Understanding loss can be a significant discovery and eliminate the fear of want. For if you want what you have, you find happiness. If you remember how important these possessions are to you, the more you treasure them, the more extraordinary. To love and remember what we had in life is the path to understanding. Don't ever turn on those who love you. Don't ever disregard what you choose to love. Reminisce on those moments we had. Hold in adoration what you are given in this life as a treasure that only you can possess. Because we will only find it here. Life is something to be appreciated. The longer we possess a love for what we have, the longer we will always enjoy it.

To understand the moment is a far more difficult thing to achieve than one would think. One always wonders should I, could I, would I. Rather than look upon what one has as a gift. A gift only found here, something to be valued in the now. Not understanding the fear of loss can lead to an unhealthy perception of the truth. To hold on is natural. Remembering what one has is how you appreciate your life. Something to always be looked upon with happiness. To not mourn what we lose, but to celebrate what we had and what we still have. These are all gifts, only found in the present. Do not look to lose but be open-minded about the value of what we hold dear.

To see clearly the moment is the only way to appreciate what we value. A lesson easily explained but harder rather to live by. To not be overwhelmed by the idea of loss, but to be invigorated by the idea of having what we hold dear is truth. Worth cannot be discounted. Only remembered. The memories we share with those we love. The experiences we want to remember can never be forgotten. So how can one lose if they live correctly? If they follow the compass and are true to what they have and hold here as humans, one can never really lose.

However, one cannot explain the loss to someone or something unless they have experienced it for themselves. But once experienced, once met, one can understand the value of what one truly has. This life is a test, a test to see if we can live it. To understand these simple truths is the path to the achievable. To remember why we can only have things for a short time is to have the ability to remember them always. To casually stumble into the future, only chasing what we cannot possess or running away from what we truly have, is a mistake. To recognize that what we have is a gift, something that cannot be taken lightly, but always cherished as something we found of value here on Earth.

We love what we have while we have it. And we remember what we had after it's gone. All things wax and wane. Our thoughts and memories are things we choose to enjoy. Enjoyment should be an essential goal, while one is here. Happiness is a choice. We should not run away from things that we are afraid to lose. Understanding is the path to contentment. To try to always show love and kindness to all is the best way to reminisce what we have found here. For the act of love, it's not what we get; it's in what we give. So, to truly understand loss is to love what we have. To dance like no one is watching, or so to speak. To take everything in as a new experience. To return favors and be generous. To not back down from a challenge simply because we are afraid to lose. To live your life with open arms because no one really knows what we may acquire here. That our lives on Earth can only be remembered by what we choose to remember is special and unforgettable. And always hold in value what we decided to keep in our hearts. Remembering what we found here as something more significant than anything else.

Because life ends, but love does not. To have a fear of loss is only a way to deny yourself the gifts that can be found here. To run away from a possibility is only denying yourself that joy. The joy of a sense of belonging, so much greater than merely fitting in.

How can one find the worth of something? We must not judge a book by its cover. Do not close yourself off from a world of significance by being afraid of knowing its value. If to have is to hold, then one must treasure what one has while they have it. To understand the worth, one must understand the loss. To understand the loss, one must lose. If, "Once bitten twice shy," How does one stay open-minded enough to want to experience anything again. Do not shut yourself off from that which you may lose. Instead open yourself to the idea that you may possess, even for a short time, a love rarely found. Something often missed, but once found it is treasured. If you don't stop and look around occasionally, you may miss it.

How important it is to look for these moments. They only last if you allow them to exist. Running from something because of a fear of losing it is a contradiction. How can you lose what you never put in the middle? Don't be afraid to go all-in, and play a hand that could have won. You will never know what wonders will become in life if you do not give them the chance to happen. To grow into a beautiful understanding of what it means to have. "Grow like a plant" is the idea. To start at the root of something and allow it to flower to fruition. To look upon and remember every petal of it. And to rightly have in one's heart a sense of genuine adoration for the experience of at some point in life having such a profound significance. To be able to look upon life and say, "YES!" I found it. What I was looking for was here all along. All I had to do was look with both eyes and see that what I truly wanted to be right in front of me. All that one must do is look at life as a place where all things are possible. Nothing is trivial. To be open to the idea that we may receive something that is of overwhelming value at any moment. Something for the spirit that can truly teach us about life. And if we are afraid of losing that for which do not have already would be cutting ourselves off at the knees.

Life is merely an opportunity to sink or swim. Fear of loss can be like swimming. One does not want to stay afloat until they have a fear of drowning. Once one understands the fear of drowning, it is easier to stay afloat. Once one knows how to float, one can swim to the other side. Once one can swim, one can always navigate a pool. Like surfing, to continually be searching for the next big wave, will guide you to the one you were meant to take.

You must look upon life in this way. Finding your own path will lead you to a real understanding of your own situation. And therefore, being able to distinguish between the wave everyone wants and the one you were meant to take. Only you can distinguish between the two.

This world is so bent on winning that most don't even play their hand. A real player takes their time. Waiting for a decent hand, and then playing it for all its worth. Life is very similar. You must play your hand. Even if you don't like the cards you've been dealt. To recognize the beauty in all things. To meet every moment like it was meant to be is a path to real success. To triumph in life is to play your hand. Who knows what you may get out of it. But to appreciate what one does attain is the path to insight. Insight is the one thing that can tell you the worth of something. You must look deep within to see what is truly in front of you. Once found, the only person who can lose it is you. So, I cherish what I have gained, I do not fear what I do not have, and I am always willing to take life on with both hands. Hold on for as long as you can…And enjoy the ride.

To lose is its own lesson; to gain is its own reward. But to find the wisdom between the two is the path to enlightenment. We all pass through life without the knowledge of what we may receive. But to be grateful for what we do have is what makes life magnificent. One must only look within to find all the love at the moment that one can achieve. To always remember what we find here on Earth. To cherish what we have. To not mourn what we do not. To pass on a message of love to all around us.

To receive the love which is given. That the moments we have, we have together. To find what is right, to set aside what is not. All one must do is look within to find the truth. When we lose, we must recollect what we still have. That we can say goodbye to what is lost and welcome what is to come. That we all are in this life together, and that we must always remember what we acquired here. It is a step in the right direction to follow this path and rejoice in what we may receive. Do not lament what we do not have. And always be complete in this understanding. Let us journey further into the realm of fear and see what we can discover.

Pain

The next fear to be aware of is the fear of pain. This does not necessarily mean just physical pain, but emotional and spiritual pain as well. To accept what you get in life is to understand why we all must go through this passage. Look upon it as a right to live life in all its mindfulness. That sometimes, we may hurt, but it is a road to a higher understanding. We all must advance into an understanding that we all must feel wounded sometimes. To understand this is the key. For whom are we if we do not examine what it is that we experience in life? The good and the bad.

To live is to hurt. To feel it is to understand who we are. To embrace our pain is to find out who we truly are. The pain we feel from what we go through in life is only a lesson. And every time we face this lesson, the more we grow. The growth into a better person. One who is always aware of oneself. That the path of pain is only an understanding of life. One we all must face. To live and learn in a larger world is in everyone's best interest. To hold oneself back from this understanding is only a charade.

A thoughtful life is a life of acceptance. It is the real road to take. And the path is not something to dissuade you from living a life of consciousness. A life of focus. The focus on a more significant existence. And everything is a part of your reality. Therefore, when others hurt you hurt, when others rejoice, you rejoice. That we are all in this together. To sympathize with those who hurt makes us more extraordinary human beings. To share in other's experiences of distress is to be human. Being human is accepting what goes on around you. To shy away from this experience is only to not receive life. Life is to be shared. And the only way to do this is through understanding. Understanding leads you closer to the truth. The truth is that we are all here for a reason. A reason to share. A reason to experience. A reason to understand. The path to understanding is not only what we face as individuals, but what we face together. To share with others our experiences is to become part of a broader concept. That there is no escaping reality. That at times we may be down, times we may be up. This is the only constant. We must cherish life when we are up, accept life when we are down. Happiness is a choice. And to rejoice in the fact that we are all here on the same road. To do what it is we must do on this path.

Pain is a natural part of our lives, and we all must do what we can to appreciate it. The fear of pain will only discourage you from the truth of our reality. That we all must hurt to understand life. People will stray from the idea of pain; they don't want to feel it. Others will strive for pain because they think that is all life is. To accept it in moderation is the key. We do not always hurt. And we are not always happy. An understanding must be found. Even if it means you are not comfortable with it. Life is full of its ups and downs. These are moments to live by. Moments to learn. We are only as great as we allow ourselves to be. Many do not allow themselves to be great.

 Many hides behind the curtain of selfishness. But to understand, to live your life according to life's rules and not your own alone, is to truly live. To aspire to greatness is no easy task. You must be willing to receive experience in the ebb and flow. To not falter in a quest for self, but rather a pursuit of an abundance of life. To seek the road less traveled. To become a human being in all its directions. To accept the unavoidability of fate, and to truly understand yourself as being a part of the eternal order of things. This world cannot be the same without you. And at the same time, you could not be who you are without this world. To share the experience of your life with others is the path to enlightenment, something we all go through... something we all must share.

Others may not want to share their pain. But in the time that binds, it is essential to at least be open to contributing sincerity to your own experience. Even if others do not. To illuminate upon others that the path to a better life is not walked alone. That no one journeys by themselves. To share one's pain is to be open to growth. Spiritual growth is the key to advancement. To be willing to share in other experiences is the key to a more meaningful existence. One must be ready to navigate into a more considerable, more global thinking. We are not alone in this life. We do not understand it without help. We may differ in how we think, but in hard times we can always count on each other for a sympathetic ear. To confide in others in time of need is to trust those around you. To hold it in is only to not allow yourself to process the pain in which you feel.

Pain is tricky because no one wants to feel it. No one wants to admit that it's there. One must share their misery before they can see it diminish. But when are you comfortable enough to share it? Whoever is closest to you should be the one to hear your lament. If you have no one to confide in, then you must look for someone to share it with. Pain cannot be dealt with alone. And to harbor your problems is to be unproductive. But we all have those in our lives that we can confide in. Use them as a source of inspiration. A means to an end. The end of your pain. The willingness to go further. When you dare to face your fear, you will be ready to move on. But this cannot be done alone. Sharing one's pain is the source of your relief. When you have done this, you will be ready to proceed.

Pain is a magnificent tool for understanding life. No one wants to feel it, no one wants to admit it. However, we all go through it. We cannot keep it bottled up forever. It will only destroy you. Nevertheless, sharing it with others is to reach a state of enlightenment that many do not find. Fear of self will defeat anyone. You must be willing to share with others what you truly feel. To harbor fear of pain will only destroy you. We are afraid to share because we do not know what reaction we will get. Will it be good, will it be bad, will we be mocked, or will we be understood? But to hold it inside of you will only extinguish your flame. Something which should burn bright. Something that should not burn out.

The only way to ensure that we grow is that we develop what we are here to become through being open enough to share it. This can create a rift between self and others if not dealt with. No one wants to admit that they have done anything wrong. No one wants to share their losses. We only want to share our triumphs. But if you take a step back, you realize that overcoming hardship is an actual victory. And victory is celebrated. All want to be a part of it. So why not share your triumph along with your defeats. To share your pain is not a loss, only a gain. To accept your situation is to succeed in life and to move on to bigger and better things.

To accept pain is to grow. To share pain is to move on. We all want to grow. We all want to live. We do not want to be trapped by life's complications. To be full, to be present, to be resolute. To live up to life's challenges and not to be afraid to share those experiences with others. To be fearless in the face of what is to come. To be brave in facing our stories. To be willing to share with others your heartache. To be willing to share in the suffering of others. This is the path to personal growth.

Something that is often sought but rarely found. You must understand that you do not go through it alone. That we all must share here what we have. Life is a gift, something to be thankful for. Do not be afraid to share your experience with others. You do not know who is out there who wants to share theirs.

For now, we must be unafraid to share our experiences with others. Perhaps one day, we will all share in the experience of a perfect humanity. Until then, we must do our best to move forward. Sharing life's experience is the only way to grow. To grow is the only path forward. To move forward is to be closer to the achievable. Chasing growth is the path. And as it is easy to stray from this path, we are all set upon it. So, we must not stray.

Personal growth is the only correct way to live. To find personal growth, we must accept others. To truly understand others is to not be afraid of what others may think. To share is to be fruitful. That fruit is a better life. We can only benefit from this. Sharing one's pains is the path to overcoming the fear of it. Extinguishing the fear of pain is to step into a larger world. One that welcomes you with open arms. To accept your fears and rise above, is the only right path to a more abundant life. If this is what you seek, then become patient with the acquisition of this lesson. And realize that it is possible for you too. Overcoming fear of pain can only aid you in your conquest of something greater than mere existence. Finding that there is something greater inside you.

To share what is truly inside us, can help guide us. If only we could live open free lives and be rewarded for it. Too many times, we are penalized for sharing our fears. Others may mock us, cast us aside. Treat you as weak. However, to truly understand how to live, then we must not hold value in hate. Truth is truth, it takes courage to rise above. To share is to rise, and those that would cast you out only stand to lose.

For we all have a soul, we all are equal. We must discover this for ourselves. And it will set you free. You will fly far above other's criticisms. You will accept yourself and all your flaws. You cannot be held down by those who do not believe in something more significant. For there is something greater.

 Understanding your fear of pain is key to advancement. Do not be afraid to get hurt. You can't lose what you don't put in the middle. Nevertheless, if you never go all in, you'll never know what you will receive. I can only show you the path. Only you can walk it. If you go through life, afraid of what might happen, you will miss what is truly there to attain. Being unafraid of pain will allow you to walk through life with your head held high. And those that would mock you only stand to lose. For we all are beautiful souls, and we all deserve the right to shine. Others will try to hold you down. Do not allow them to debase your being. If more knew the path, more would take it. Sadly, most do not know the path.

You will see that once you begin the path, the more excellent person you will become. Stand tall in your journey along the road to enlightenment. Walk through life with your shoulders back and your head held high. I guarantee you will be glad you did. Like cream, you will rise to the top. Those who used to mock you will want to be like you. Those who cast you aside will only want what you have. Then you will see what there is for you. To be able to live a life and lead the way to truth and happiness, not only for yourself but for others. Pain is nothing more than an obstruction in the way of living a fruitful life. And being afraid of that pain will only blind you from what is truly there— a life of success and contentment.

Suffering

The next fear in line would be suffering. Like the great Buddha taught, there is a way beyond suffering. It is something that must be experienced. It must be faced throughout our very lives. Sorrow comes, and it goes. To not lose yourself to it is the key. The "Four noble truths" that the Buddha taught was a plan on how to overcome suffering. It begins by accepting that everyone suffers, and finding the path to overcome suffering is possible. That you only suffer as much as you let yourself suffer. It is inescapable. We all suffer—no two ways about it. However, you can learn how to deal with it. Even to a point where you no longer fear suffering again. We all want, we all are afraid to lose, we all don't want to feel pain. Now we must realize that suffering is also a basic fear. The path to enlightenment is in learning that one can only suffer as much as one lets themselves suffer. Some use drugs and alcohol to avoid suffering. However, this only delays the inevitable. To run from a fear of hell can only delay your descent to madness. Suffering is one of the most potent fears. One cannot advance in life without facing it. And we all face it every day.

There is no end to suffering, but we can accept it and move on. Or we can let it linger, and it will destroy us. Accepting the source of your suffering is the beginning. Realizing that you are not the only one who suffers comes next. Letting the suffering go is the finish line. Once you have acquired this knowledge, you can face fear a thousand times. Each time you successfully meet the fear of suffering, the easier it becomes to face it again. Many are not ready for this. We distract ourselves. We ran and hide from it. There are plenty of things to lose yourself in. We can only delay the unavoidability of facing the same suffering again. There is only one way through the fear of suffering. So, the choice is yours. You must endure to overcome a fear of suffering. As much as you don't want to admit it, suffering is a fact of life. You can only hold yourself back from the progress you can achieve by not facing it. Don't get me wrong, suffering is one of the most powerful forces one can face in one's time here on Earth. We distract ourselves. We run and hide from it. There are plenty of things to lose yourself in. Everyone goes through it. It is up to you how you want to deal with it. Decide as an individual how you want to live your life. Running and hiding from the truth or standing up to follow a higher path. You don't need religion. Only the understanding that we all go through it. So many run and hide, so many never face it. To learn this lesson now is one of the most incredible things you can do for yourself. To start right now, for yourself, an understanding how to deal with your suffering. This is incredibly beneficial to one's own sanity. Overcoming this fundamental value of self will only propel you into the type of person you always wanted to become. If doing what is most beneficial is your goal, then heed these instructions. Facing one's fears is the only way to overcome them. Overcoming them is the key to a larger world. However, you must take the first step into this new world on your own. You must first find the courage to go through it. Is it achievable? The answer is, "Yes!" And there are few things greater than attaining this knowledge. It will set you free. It is so easy to just run and hide from the truth. Nevertheless, you will eventually have to face it. Face your fears. The longer you take in obtaining this knowledge, the longer it will take to grow as a human being.

To conquer one's thoughts allows one to triumph in the face of all those who suffer. It feeds the soul. And every time you face your suffering, the better you will get at it. This should drive one to stand up and take it. Take back control over one's own self, and the direction it is going in. You can go in any direction you want. However, eventually, you will have to face the fact that there is only one, "True North." Upon the Great Compass is where you will find yourself. You will feel more comfortable moving in some directions over others. But to deny the fact that there is a path to life is to your own advantage.

 The fear of suffering is so powerful that some escape civilization ultimately, just to discover this path. And this path has been searched for, for thousands of years. Entire religions have been based on it. However, beliefs can be deceiving. The only truth is that you must find it for yourself. You cannot acquire it without understanding this simple fact. It is easy to be told the path, but you can only discover it by facing it head-on. No amount of teaching can alleviate it from your life. The fear of suffering is embedded in our existence. One only must climb the mountain and see the view from above. To gaze down upon your fears and realize at that moment that you have overcome them. At this moment, you will find what you've been looking for all along. To face it again is merely another mountain to climb.

Do not be confused with the engagements of the masses. Looking for enlightenment there will only confuse you. As religion is "the Opiate for the masses," so is trying to find the truth in the crowd. It will not happen. One should make personal growth a goal in life. And overcoming suffering should be one of those goals. You will be able to look upon your life with clarity. You will be able to overcome the truth of our reality. That suffering is ever-present. It will never go away.

However, how you deal with it can alleviate this issue. That we all suffer, nevertheless we can overcome and become more fantastic human beings by doing so. You will never forget what makes you suffer. And you can always remember how you deal with it. It is an excellent decision to learn how to deal with it. The longer you dwell, the more effort it takes to overcome. Some seek counseling, some try to find the solution in the crowd. All well and good, the only place you'll find the answer is within yourself. You must seek it with your very soul. You must focus your energy on a manner that defeats the suffering. You will only thank yourself for doing so.

There is only one real path to take. When you understand how to navigate your compass, you can find your way on the map. How great life could be if we all knew this simple truth. To continually grow and achieve a greater self in our lives should be our goal here. You can face any obstacle, climb any mountain, swim to any depth. And always return to the point of, "True North." How fantastic life could be if everyone knew this. Some know and choose to avoid it. No one wants to be told what to do. To be open-minded enough to accept simple instruction, to be taught any lesson. It is the path to personal enlightenment. To become a student, you must receive a teacher. Until you understand what has been introduced, you cannot comprehend. When you have faced your fear, you can face it a thousand times. The more you do it, the better you are at navigating your worries. Facing fears is the base to higher means of living. Once you understand this, the less you'll dwell on the fear that you have. In this case, it would be suffering. The only way to overcome suffering is to understand why we suffer. This will lead you to the pathway of insight. To look within oneself is an ability. Something to value. Something to guide us. Something to learn and be taught. How great life could be for everyone to understand how to deal with this fear. Nonetheless, we all must struggle with it until we have learned it. Until everyone understands this truth, we must all strive to do our best to alleviate these fears. To be open-minded enough to help others find the same. And for all to coexist in a manner that reflects our understanding of it. This is the goal; this is the key—the key to a lock that will reveal a most beneficial future. To find the key and unlock the door. See what is beyond the threshold.

Change

Next, we come to the fear of change. No one wants to stand out. Nobody wants to be left behind. To enact a change in yourself takes discipline. Just as trying something new can be revealing. Being able to change is a sign of growth. To be able to grow can only benefit. Even though many would like to run and hide. Seeing the truth will only set you free. Change is unavoidable. The simple truth is everything changes. To welcome that change puts you on a higher path, the path to enlightenment. Like any animal, the ability to adapt to one's surroundings is a tool to survival. Being able to adjust to one's environment is necessary for life. Therefore, trying to hide behind this truth is only detrimental to one's continued reality. There will be things in your life that will cloud your vision. There will be things that elude you.

To recognize the higher path is to acknowledge that things change. Change should be welcomed. Our thinking should be challenged. To adapt to your situation is beneficial to you. To be aware of one's surroundings is the ability to navigate one's pathway. The direction to spiritual growth comes from accepting one's perception. Situations will arise when you must face the truth. To accept this as a fact of life will only assist you in your spiritual goal. To rise above the challenges that you face. To expand your sights upon your objectives is only the beginning. To accept the truth that nothing lasts forever will only make you appreciate your situation more. In any circumstance, the ability to adapt to your present condition is most beneficial to you. Your spiritual growth. To your ascension to a higher existence. If higher realities are your goal, then accepting change is necessary for personal growth.

Everyone wants things to stay the way they are. Especially when times are good. When life is going your way. No one wants terrible times. To direct one's goals in the sight of facing change is the ability to lead. To be able to lead yourselves on the route is to find true happiness. To be able to teach others is the path to success. However, you must accept the fact that things do not stay the way they are forever. To adapt to one's situation is the ability to transcend. To grow and surpass an existence far beyond your imagination. And all that you may envision is the life that you want it to be. Imagine understanding this and being able to teach it to others. How much they could benefit from this knowledge. However, many do not want to be awakened from their delusion. That we are all fixed, that there is no escape. That we are all stuck on an absolute path that we cannot evade. Only a disillusioned path to the self that is distorted by the objectives of the crowd. To bow down to the ordinary is to forfeit the life of the extraordinary.

However, there is a way to rise above our unsatisfactory life situation. Do not fear growing spiritually in the eyes of the community. To stand out may be uncomfortable, but to travel the path to truth, there can be little penalty. Many will try and hold you back. But if your quest is self-enlightenment, then understanding this fact is to meet the challenge head-on. A spiritual awakening unlike any you have ever experienced. Something that will set you apart from the rest. So many do not want change to not occur. They want to hide upon a route that never distinguishes itself from the ordinary. However, some want the extraordinary. To understand this reality is to appreciate how much those who do not welcome change are ever drawn to it. Most do not realize that the ability to deal with change is a self-advancing practice. For those that have it is a navigational instrument, for those that don't have it, a crutch. To always strive for truth is the essence of achieving. Being able to accept change and move on is the path to a higher reality. Nothing stays the same. There is always movement. A body in motion stays in motion. Energy can never be defeated, only redirected. To be able to move and navigate through life is the awareness of this change. Like a river with many twists and turns, the flow will always guide you upon your journey. Let it guide you upon the path. Let yourself welcome every twist and turn on your voyage. And as you traverse the rivers channel, let you always know your way. The way to true enlightenment. The path to illumination. The path to the achievable.

The direction of "True North," is for you to guide yourself upon. Accepting change is a measure of one's ability to pilot their soul through life. That standing up to a challenge rather than running away from it is the path to confidence. The certainty that can only be found by one's owns ability to search for this simple truth. The truth that comes from discovery. Which can only be found upon the path to a higher reality. This inescapable truth. When you search for it, it will always be found. "Lift a stone and you shall find it, split a piece of wood and I am there. " When you are aware of this truth, that all things change, that the only constant thing is change itself. The only thing that can hold you back is your unwillingness to deal with this change. To grow stagnant will only delude you from the truth of reality. That all things transform, and there is no way around it. To develop and accept the idea that everything is always changing is the path to self. That self-truth is the only certainty. And to be certain, one must be willing to grow and move with these changes. Nothing is constant. And wanting things to never change is its own loss. So, it really comes down to one thing. Do you want to win or lose in life? Those who succeed are those who accept change, and there are those who do not. It is up to you. All I can do is bring light to the idea, you are the one who must accept it. Upon this path, I wish for you only truth. I hope you go on in life to stand up to every obstacle. And let your soul be relieved that there is a method beyond all the madnesses. This understanding comes with the acceptance that the world is always turning and that there is no fixed position. Nothing is static. That accepting change is a fact of life. That all that you face in life allows you to grow. That you can walk yourself in a better direction. Something which changes your life forever. And forever, your life might be changed. With every step you grow, your life will develop with you. To understand the truth of change can only benefit you in the revolving world. To know that every change you feel here on Earth is a path to growth. To grow is to enlighten. Enlightenment is achievable. And in your search for the achievable, you will only benefit from this teaching. Accepting change as a part of life is the only way to exist. People fear change for many reasons. Some want only to conform. To fit in. However, some search for more. Knowing that there is a way, and that way is accessible, is all you really need to know. The only way is to realize that our path has many twists and turns and that it is our voyage. I can open the door, but you are the one who must walk through it. Sometimes change is easy, sometimes it is hard. There is no way to escape it. You can run from it your whole life and get nowhere. Nevertheless, you will have to face it eventually. Open your mind to change. Live a fruitful life. Live to satisfy your soul. To strengthen the mind. To open one's heart. So instead of hiding from this simple truth, accept change and proceed upon the path that has been set before you. Then you will see that change is to be welcomed. And that passage begins here.

Not Having Enough

The next fear in the long line of fears is the fear of not having enough. To protect ourselves and what we have is an instinct. We all experience it. To be able to defend what we have is natural. Perhaps we always will want more out of life. But to preserve what we have is a predisposition to supporting our existence. The fear of not having enough can allow us to treasure what we do have. To keep what we have and to protect it is a natural tendency. To defend that which we already have is the aim that we all set upon our own reality. No one wants to lose, however, not being able to keep what one already has can be defined as fear. To not have enough could scare anyone into an antagonistic state. Not having enough will only drive you to want more. But to truly accept wanting more is to only understand what we do not have already. It is hard to say what is most important. But to be human, we must take that which we can understand and mold it into something we can utilize. Things that we do not want to lose. Things we want to hold on to. That we will rise to the occasion of defending these assets. I'm not materialistic, but I am always on the search for more. We work hard for the things we have and do not want to lose them. So, fear of not having enough is an obstacle in our path to self-truth. How we live and preserve our rights as humans, is what we call our reality. To rise above and accept our way, is to recognize our humanity. To understand that there are things we keep, and there are things we lose, is a natural state of being. To stand up for that which we already have is our right as human beings. To emerge above it all and accept what is given us is the path. To protect what we have is the goal. To defend what is ours is completely inherent. It's not that we want more, it's that we don't want to lose what we already have. We will fear that we don't have enough, however it does not mean we do not possess what we need. We safeguard what we at present have. We defend it with our very lives. For those that we love, we defend what is theirs, and hope for the best. The fear of not having enough is plenty enough to be a concern. How are we ever to achieve something higher than the essential self of human existence, without wanting more. We all do it, we all want it. To uphold what we have is a straightforward method to self-achievement. However, this is not a matter of greed, only a matter of self-preservation. To stay constant for the things we love is a definite goal in life. We do not want the ones we hold dear to go wanting. We guard that which we possess. And for fear of not having enough, it should be something we strive for. No one wants to lose, no one wants to not have enough. So, we go through life trying to accomplish the goal of having ample resources to sustain an existence. An existence that is based upon a maintainable supply of assets. Achievable assets, assets that can provide us with the necessary collection of spiritual as well as tangible benefits in our lives.

To be afraid of not having enough is a roadblock to self-preservation. It can only haunt you into thinking that you need more. However, it is merely an obstacle. You do not need more you do not need less. To understand that we all have things that we are afraid of losing is a reality check. To want more is a difficulty. But to be happy with what one has is truth. We protect our belongings, our possessions. With our very lives, we hold dear to that which we most cherish. We don't want to lose what we have. To be grateful for this sets us above the rest. Some things are intangible. To defend that which we hold true is human. One does not need more, only a recognition of what one has. In this world, it is hard to find the truth. And in that, it is hard to distinguish what is truly real and what is not. Somethings you possess are not always tangible. No one can take that away from you. To stand up for and cherish that which you have is the path to illumination. To want more is a deception. So, in fact, the fear of not having enough is a mere roadblock in your goal of ascension. Your ascension into a larger world. It is not necessarily understanding what you have or what you want, only what you want to secure. And in this, the fear of not having enough appears. What you are left with is what you truly have. To be grateful for what you have is the path to truth. And the truth will set you free. So do not be afraid of not having enough. Be aware of your surroundings, and always stand up for what you believe in. And you will be right in your life. To be right with your life is the aim. And to let go of this fear of not having enough is a key to your open-minded reality. So be grateful for what you have, do not grieve for which you do not. Your life will be yours, and no one can take it from you. You will be able to move on in life without fear of those who would try to harm you. And the ability to protect that which you already have will become clear. So, proceed with this knowledge and conquer your fears, you will never have more than you are meant to have. And those things you are meant to have will truly be yours. Respect what you have, do not mourn what you have not. Navigate through life less selfishly. You will only be better for it.

Life

What comes next is a fear of life. A fear of life can be daunting. Perhaps we are scared to experience it. Maybe we had a rough time in life and do not want to go on. To walk through life afraid of living is detrimental to our wellbeing. We must be willing to accept life on life's terms. We must wake up every day eager to take life head-on. To be prepared to confront our daily battles. To rise to the challenge. To climb the next hill, and not to stop till we reach the top. Fearing what comes next is no way to go through life. We all have reasons to be afraid of what comes next. But to let it slow us down in our life's journey is harmful thinking. Sometimes we must stand up for what we believe in. Conquering a fear of life is truly an achievement, it is something to be proud of. To be able to wake up each morning with a sigh of relief. That a new day will be better than the old one. To face our fears and rise to the occasion. To impress upon oneself that we can do it. We can stand up to anything. That we can accomplish any task. Once you come to this realization, you will be amazed at what your life becomes. You will walk through life with a sense of accomplishment. To face one's personal battles head-on is the goal. Once you've done it once, you can do it a thousand times. Be courageous and stand up for what you believe in, and you will be amazed by the time you are done. Others will look up to you, you will have a new sense of happiness in your life. You will actively become a part of the mainstream without fear of what others may think. Things that used to baffle you will become routine endeavors. The more you stand up to your fears, the more you realize that there is nothing to worry about.

The only thing that holds you back from living the life that you want to live in, is your fear of doing so.

To come to the realization that the only way to go through life is to face things head-on. It is all one needs to know about acquiring the essential components to living a life of conscience. Do not run from the uncertainties of life. You may discover that it was nothing to fear at all. Facing these concerns in life should bring a smile to your face. Not a frown of not being strong enough to face them. You can only hold yourself back in life. The sooner you learn this lesson, the better. To cower to life's challenges will only bring you down. However, to rise to the occasion will be a proven success for one's own self-worth. If spiritual growth is your goal, then you can only gain from facing this challenge. Things will appear to you in life that used to confuse you. At first glance, things may seem too difficult. Going through life with your head held low is its own downfall. You can only defeat yourself. However, to walk through reality with your head held high is its own victory. You will feel like you can do anything. This kind of personal insight is crucial to conquering one's doubts. It is a step closer to navigating your spiritual and moral compass and setting yourself upon the path of, "True North."

You must face your fears of life to live the life you want to lead. You must conquer your personal battles. You must let your soul soar to new heights. Once you do, you will fly like an eagle, high above the Earth. You will become untouchable. Things that you were once afraid of will disappear. You will see life through bifocal lenses. You will be ready for the big show. The curtain before you open, and you will be center stage. A sense of success will overwhelm you. Doubts and worries will disappear from your feet. Every step of your life will be a new path to personal growth. Soon conflict and how to deal with it will vanish. Only an incredible sense of self will remain. Your life's finally begun, and there will be no more hiding from the simple truth. The truth of life is to stand tall, be healthy, and welcome all adversity.

Conquering a fear of life will create an awareness of one's situation. You will know who you are and where you stand. The overwhelming sense of dread will disappear. The clouds will part, and you will see the sun in all its glory. The path to the achievable will become known to you. A step in the right direction will lead you upon this path and will strengthen your senses. You will know what it is like to truly belong to the world, in all its wonder. This path is attainable. To begin this journey, one must merely take a deep breath, smile, and take a step. Let your inhibitions disappear and a sense of self will take over. A true sense of self. Confident, and strong. This will alleviate you with a sense of self-liberation. You will begin to see the world how it is meant to be seen without the fear of life. This is one of the most empowering feelings known to man. So do not stray from the path of, "True North." Use your compass, and navigate yourself to the path of enlightenment, a way free of fear. You can only gain from this teaching. And you will never be the same again.

Death

And now we come to the final fear-Death. It is natural to fear death. However, we all must face it. Death is certain, life isn't. Even though we do not know what comes after, we can face this fear on our own two feet. Life is a beautiful thing. So, to cherish what we have and experience life to its fullest is the essential way to conquer this fear. The fear of death can overcome anyone. Death is a scary thing. We hide ourselves from it. We try to avoid thinking about it. However, everyone dies. How we deal with this part of our journey is up to us. Choose life. Choose happiness.

Living a life of mindfulness will allow one to look at death from a new perspective. As we grow older, we can either run from this fact of life or embrace it. To perceive death correctly is to welcome what is to come. To not accept this fundamental truth is to not flourish in life. So, to run from this fact of life is to not enjoy what we have when we have it. Facing one's fear of death will allow you to look at life with cognizant eyes. You will learn to value your experiences more and more. You will evaluate and appreciate your time here with greater perspective. Materialism will fade away. Your relationships with others will improve drastically. The superfluous distractions in life will seem of less value. You will be one with your emotions. You will begin to feel more human. The shroud that has been pulled over your eyes will be removed. All other fears will subside, and you will be left with an understanding that is more human.

We share in the certainty that death must be faced. This understanding is crucial to living a spiritual life. It is a hard thing to contemplate. We can run from it all our lives. However, we all must face it. Death is something we all share. Even though we must face it alone. We share an existence with all living things. This idea should bring some comfort. This is the proper way to face the fear of death. And though we mourn those who leave this life, we must feel comfort in their memory. And that they will always be treasured. To love and be loved in the closeness we share. This eases the passing of time and the relationships we experience.

To be able to appreciate life comes from an understanding of death. The fear of death is perceived and undergone in different ways. Some run from it, some run to it. Death should be welcomed but not pursued. This is only a lesson to be learned. Hopefully you come to this understanding before you face it. Life is short and precious. It is something to be celebrated. It should warm the heart. Welcoming our fate will only make our lives more wonderful. It is inevitable. One day we all will lose. But does this mean we shouldn't care? I think not. Chasing death, or not loving life is the wrong outlook. We all can determine how we deal with the fear of death. Recognizing that we all share this life is a good attitude. Whether there is something after death is irrelevant. Don't get me wrong, I believe in an afterlife. But not focusing on the present will only allow you to overlook the moment. To always treasure what we have here. To live and be loved. To experience all we can. This is the appropriate way to live a life of substance. Sounds great. Is it possible? Yes! It is. You may fall, only to get back up. You may not be able to fly at the start. But if you try, try again. You may one day soar.

Master this fear, and you will live a more profound existence. You will see with soft eyes. You will love what you have. Not suffer from what you do not. You will welcome the future with open arms and open eyes. You will accept your place in this world. You will not run from conflict. You will stand up for what you believe in. You will hold dear and be true to your heart. You will be willing to let go of yesterday. Have the courage to welcome tomorrow. And the strength to live for today. Live your life by this principle and you can't go wrong. Follow this concept every day, and you will be on the path to spiritual enlightenment, and the achievable. Follow the path, and when you leave this world, you'll be the better for it.

Emotion

"The best and most beautiful things in the world cannot be seen or even touched. They must be felt with the heart."

Helen Keller

The next realm we are going to explore is emotion. It is more advanced than fear. Fears are instinctual. Emotions are feeling based. Feelings are responsive to thought. Fears drive thought. Thought drives emotions. Emotions are more unstable; they can shape our behaviors drastically. Emotions can get out of control. They can push us to borders we do not want to experience. Many gaze upon emotions as a sign of weakness. However, they are unavoidable. How we deal with them is what makes us who we are. One can try to avoid them. Nevertheless, they are always there. Dealing with them head-on is the only way to conquer them. So, as they are looked upon as a weakness, it is merely how we deal with them that shows strength. People do not want to seem weak. Most emotions are rarely even confronted. To not tackle your feelings is a dramatic flaw in our nature. Society will make you think that you should ignore your feelings. It is looked upon as a sign of helplessness. However, truly understanding your feelings is the only strong point. You will always feel emotion, we all go through it. So, to let others dictate how to live is a misconception. Taking the time to face our emotional state is the path to elevating your life. Where once others saw weakness, they will see strength. Your ability to deal with life will become a personally accepted path to the truth.

Understanding and dealing with one's emotions is bedrock to success in life. Others will look upon you in a new way. Instead of vulnerability, they will see vigor. Instead of a lack of humanity, they will see your altruism. They will recognize you as a leader, and a truth of our humanity. You will succeed as others have failed. You will rise as others fall. You will be respected for taking life head-on. And by yourself, you will recognize the truth of our existence. That we all must face our feelings. And to deal with them directly takes courage.

Emotions are inescapable, we all must face them. To not meet them only can deteriorate your life. To step up to the challenge of facing them is the path to insight. Others will try to fool you into thinking that you should just ignore your feelings. But then you would only become one of the invisible masses. Lost in a crowd of people trying to hide from the truth of reality. That reality is facing one's emotions. Like you have faced your own fears. Many things will spawn emotions. Fear more than anything. We must learn how to face our fears and accept our feelings as a part of life. No one can do it, but you. Others will try to steer you from it. Mostly from a selfish point of view for not having faced it themselves. Others will try to drag you down for their own inability to meet them also.

The truth to life is one cannot grow until one has faced opposition. The opposition comes from all those who would seek to have you fail. The only real way to find the truth is to stand up as oneself and face that which is in front of them. Like I said, others will try to hold you back. Mostly because they have not accomplished their own goals in life. No one wants to lose. But if you don't stand up for yourself, you will only lose with the rest of them. You must stand up and accept life on life's terms. To do this, one must first recognize what one faces. Once you understand what you face, you must have a calm mind. A calm mind is to be present. And to be present is to be aware.

 The ability to accept what is in front of you is the basis for all life. To keep moving forward is the goal. To not restrain oneself from the truth is the highway to a vaster reality. This presence is meant to propel you into the next dimension of thinking. Once you have realized that emotions are natural. That we all feel them. That it is not a weakness. Instead, a path to something greater. Emotions are tricky. But once you learn that the only way to face them is to experience them, you will understand a larger part of what it means to be human. To be human is the goal. So, you must understand as much about being human as you can.

The ability to deal with one's emotions makes you a stronger individual. You must have the discipline to take life head-on. If not for yourself, but for those around you. It will make you a representation of the truth. That all can accomplish excellence. And it all starts with one's ability to deal with the real. To assume that emotions are something trivial is a delusion. We all must face them. And the way we face them is up to us. So, for you to continue upon this path of enlightenment, you must understand the risks. Only to be followed by the rewards. The fact that you can overcome this takes a minute of acceptance. To be able to navigate through emotion is a strength like no other. You will stand out; you will be seen. Others will be baffled by your ability to deal with the absolution of emotion. They will wonder where you found the ability. And you can merely reply, "Within myself." Others will want to follow. However, as much as you would like to teach others, all you can teach is that it is found within.

Conquering emotion is going to lead you upon the path to awareness. Once you have obtained it, it will forever be at your disposal. The challenge of feeling emotions will no longer become an obstacle but a daily accomplishment. To overcome this obstacle is to be human. To be human is the goal. And this goal should summarize our very lives. So that we may live our lives to the fullest. So, welcome the adversity of life, embrace its challenges. Face life head-on. Accept what is in front of you. Do not deny your emotions. However, be willing to express them in a healthy manner.

 Join a more meaningful existence and be willing to feel your emotions and share them with others. Rise high to the challenge of belonging to a larger world. Make your presence here on Earth known. Do not be afraid to be human. And here as a human you will find yourself. Not alone, but part of a greater reality. To proceed and continue moving through life with the knowledge of what you have acquired. This is the basic human concept. Do not go astray into the future. However, step forward with life on life's terms. If we all must face emotions, then what is there to fear in doing so? Is it because we get lost in doing what others are doing. Or is it a loss from denying yourself to coexist in a broader perception of life. A new window to look out of. To be able to look at life through life's eyes. To accept that we are no better than anyone else. This is the path to a higher existence. This immensity of personal growth is necessary for life on a grander scale. You will no longer be held down by those around you. You will find a new sense of self. One of which you could not conceive of before. Others will look to you for guidance. You will become the teacher, and others will become the student. That which bewildered you will now become apparent. That the only one who judges you is yourself. After reaching such a state of mind, you will realize that all things are possible. Things that used to bother you will slip from your reality. You will know how to deal with your life head-on. Emotions will become merely a minor obstacle in your path. People will marvel at your ability to deal with life. You will become an example of how to live.

Hope

The first and most important emotion that we feel is hope. Hope is the quintessential basis of all other emotions. To feel hope is to be set free. That our lives and experiences will get better. That we do not live and die in vain. That there is a light that shines at the end of the tunnel. That the bad does not outweigh the good. To have hope is to wake up every day with the feeling of optimism. An optimism that everything is going to be alright. That no matter what happens, we will be okay. To accept life on life's terms and live our lives according to how we want to live them. To not give up in a world of conflict. To bring a spiritual approach to a world of uncertainty.

To deny hope is to weaken one's spirit. We need a strong soul to triumph over life. To rise to the occasion. To be ready for what life brings. To stand and deliver. We all can do so. So why do people suffer from a lack of hope? Imagine a world where we all lack the courage to face life. We would get nothing done. Or to let others bear the burden alone would be an act of cowardice. We all must coexist the best we can. So, we must all work together for a common goal. To join with each other in such a way as to share mutual hope, and this is how to succeed in life. The more we strive to live with hope in our hearts, the more we convey a sense of optimism to others. It is to be victorious in life. Imagine if everyone shared this belief. How great life would be. However, some are lost. Some don't want to face this truth. That there is hope. If this wasn't true, how senseless life would be? Envision a world in which no one believed in anything. What a pointless reality that would be.

We must stand together with a sense of hope. We must share our hope with others. We must convince others that there is such a thing. We must strive to be positive, no matter what we face. To believe that we can make a difference in our own lives as well as others. Hope is essential to growth.

Spiritual growth is the main goal in life. So why do people stray from the path? How insignificant some must feel. If only they knew the truth. That hope is good for the soul. That the balance of good and evil is found in the spirit. This balance is controlled by how we live our lives. So why not take the spiritual path. Hope is good for the soul; hope makes us smile. Hope gives strength to others. Hope lifts us up. We are better people when we are hopeful. We believe that anything is possible. It's a candle in the dark. A guiding light. So that all who are lost can see. However, many are not ready to turn on the light. So how do we show them the way? You can only teach a willing student. Nothing can be learned if the pupil isn't ready. So where do we go from here? For us to find a more meaningful existence, we need to search for that light. A light that shines bright. So that we all can illuminate our own path. For us to all light our own candles. To be our own lights in the darkness. Hopefully, others who are lost will see the light and find the truth. And let them be better people for it. If we all worked together, there would be no doubt. Hope is real, hope is great. Hope can change your life. You can only benefit from the idea of hope.

If this is all true, how can one lose hope? So, what is the problem? How can we move forward without it? It's as simple as putting one foot in front of the other. A surefooted way through life. Hope is, "True North." So how can one not see what is forever constant? Hope is eternal. Hope is achievable. So how can we miss it? It is so easy to look at the night sky and see the North Star. Having it direct you to your destination. The path to the soul is the same. To follow hope is to guide your humanity. It will always be there to lead you. Upon the way, we walk with hope in our hearts. To share this hope is to change one's reality. It can bring light to a dark world. So many who do not have hope could benefit from this light. A lantern to guide their way. For all to find the path. This road we all walk upon is a pathway of hope. One cannot grow without it. Hope is the essence of discovery. To have it is to soar high above the Earth. Things that were so hard before, now seem small at such heights. You shall float over your obstacles and see clearly the path from above.

Things that used to confuse you will seem simple. The weight of the world will not be so heavy. Your ability to navigate through life will become easier. The hope you feel will brighten your days. You will be a light for others. They will see you as a portrait of spiritual success. Your ability to guide yourself will become an instinctual concept. The darkness will subside and reveal a brilliant light—one for all to see. You will understand life from a different view. It will be natural for you to accomplish things that once seemed impossible. Your soul will be strengthened, and your vigor renewed. You will stand tall and be able to face new obstacles. Your soul will bathe in the light of the sun and glow in the moon's illumination. Your spirit will radiate with warmth for all to feel. Others will want what you have. They will look to you for guidance. Where once others ignored you, now they will notice. The ability to guide your spirit is to lead others to do the same. As you walk through life, do so upon the path to hope. Light your candle and hold it high. For all to see. For all to follow. You will be amazed at yourself as you traverse the world with a sense of confidence. The confidence you can only get through hope.

Doubt

After hope comes doubt. One of the most challenging emotions you must deal with is doubt. One will question all the things that they have to face in life. You will ponder giving up. The feeling that you have already lost. Facing the emotion of doubt is quite dumbfounding. How can one have hope if we only doubt? We all wander through life, wishing things would work out for us. But we go through life doubting what will happen. Never knowing what might occur. We have a yearning for positivity in our lives. But are often faced with the undesirable. As much as we want things to be the way we want them to be, sometimes some things do not always work as we want them to. You can either try to look at life in a positive manner or a negative one. You may hope, or you may doubt. The choice is up to you. To walk through life with your head held high or bent low. To believe that life can be better, or that life could be worse. We all want things in life. Is it better to hope for the best or count on the worst? The choice is up to you. Either way, you will eventually have to graduate your thinking into a greater perspective on life. You will ultimately get to the next stage in dealing with your emotions. It is natural to expect the worst and hope for the best. Humans are built this way. We conduct ourselves in a manner that is comfortable for us. We do not want things to change, but we accept them when they do. We must face our struggles. We wonder what life will bring. But we must meet it head-on. To go through life doubting is consuming. However, the goal in life is to progress. So, whatever makes you happy, is the path that you should take. To believe that life can be better is the brighter path. To continually doubt your position in life will only let you down. Either way, the future is coming. One way or another you will have to face reality. All things will eventually merge with your perception of life. So how you want to meet it is up to you. To be hopeful is the better course. To walk around with your head held low is its own defeat. You will find that life is so much more agreeable when you think positively. That you can face any obstacle. That no matter what happens in life, you are ready for it and can face it head-on. To doubt is to lose on a grand scale. To think positive is better.

Something that can lead you through life is a hope for a brighter future. To doubt only negates this. It will fool you into thinking that life cannot get any better. But the truth is, life only shines as bright as you want it to. We only take on what we think we can handle. So, going through life doubting will only bring a polluted point of view. However, positively looking upon life will lead to success. The higher you hold yourself, the more successful you will be. Negatively looking upon life can only lead to a disadvantage. The question is, would you instead look at life on the bright side, or go through life looking at the downside? One's approach to life is as important as anything else. We all want the best and don't want to think about the worst. But to prepare for the worst and hope for the best is one of the most significant understandings we can reach. To hope for the best means to meet life's challenges, and what comes before you to welcome what comes your way. To stand up to life's trials. Not to bow down to the encounters one must face. To test life on life's terms.

To not hesitate in the face of adversity. You can only gain from overcoming doubt. In the light of all you do, looking on the brighter side can only benefit you. To smile upon your fate and accept what you are given, is the lighter side of life. To go through life expecting the worst will only lead to your downfall. How can you see all the good things you see in life if your head is held down? To control one's doubt is to welcome life. To accept life is to take things as they are. To take things as they are, is the way to learn. To learn is to be great. To be great is to accept life. To do this is to succeed in life.

Faith

Faith is perhaps one of the more powerful positive emotions. It can endow us with a guiding light like nothing else on Earth. It is a lantern in the darkness. If we have it, we can accomplish anything. To have faith in yourself is to believe you can climb any mountain. That you can swim any ocean. That you can rise to any occasion. Faith is.

It is not putting faith into something; It is putting faith into yourself. To recognize the strength in self is to conquer the world. It is the power to lead armies. With faith, others will look upon you with awe. They will wonder where you got your confidence. They will want what you possess. Others will be baffled by your ability to take on life. Things that once gave you difficulties will seem to become less challenging. You will navigate through life with ease. The amount of self-worth you acquire through faith is immeasurable.

Such a belief in self can only be experienced through one's modern interpretations of life. First, you need to see it. Then you need to be it. The way you look upon life will change. Things will seem less intimidating. Like David, you will conquer the Goliath. Your worries will melt away, and you will become strong enough to meet any conflict. Your daily efforts will be doubly rewarded. You will understand what it means to be a leader. And your army will be those you touch with your confidence. They will look upon you with admiration. They will want what you have. This will make you even greater than before. You will understand life through a new outlook. You will take life on and realize that success is merely an attitude. And attitude is success. It will become merely a reference point for you. Faith will become your tool for supporting your heart and all your emotions. Something steady. Something you can count on. To put faith into self will be your shield in hard times. It will be your sword in a life of uncertainty. You will ride upon life, and faith will be your steed. You will know about new levels of confidence. It will become something you can share with others that will only empower them. Then they will see life through new eyes as well.

Faith will guide you. Once this is understood, there is no going back. You must embrace it as a powerful tool. Or dread it in fear of success. Some people are afraid of accomplishment. They don't want to know that they are good enough to have true faith. This is more reason to have a strong belief. Because it is real. The ones who have it already are ready to take on the world. And the ones who are afraid only hold themselves back. All it takes is one moment of self-assurance to show anyone how to do it. To put faith in oneself is a learning experience. Meaning it is teachable. And the great teachers of all time understood it. They were conduits of faith. They taught that it is possible to live life with faith and be better for it. They believed it so much that they changed the world. What kind of leader wouldn't want their citizens to have faith. Which is why the greatest of teachers taught it. So that you would rise above. You will improve upon others with your ability to guide yourself. Rather than be ruled by your lack of a positive attitude. This has been the pattern for so long that many are lost to the idea of faith. They just accept that things are the way they are, and you can't do anything about it. I am here to say, "No!" This is not the way. You must believe in yourself. You must rise above. You must climb that mountain. You must find faith in yourself.

We can all teach those without faith how to have it. Then one day, we shall be better for it. We will encourage each other to possess a positive attitude. We will impact upon our children the influence of conviction. And they will teach their children. Until all understand the power of faith. We will educate those around us to believe in themselves. A true self. A self that understands that to accomplish the impossible is to believe that you can. To not cower or cater to the negative. To embrace an optimistic mind. To focus on a successful life is to have the faith enough to live it. Those who see your radiance within their hearts will be transformed by it.

The eternal balance of life and the achievable is determined by how we live our lives. To have faith in self is to guide one's soul. Energy cannot be defeated, only redirected. So how we direct our energy is how far we come in life towards what is truly achievable. We can only strengthen our souls to go the distance. How far we come in life is as close to that accomplishment as we can get. Can it be accomplished in a lifetime? I say to you, "Yes!" Anything is possible. So do not wander through life without faith as your guide. You will only be better for it. So, upon this journey, remember, hold your head high, and have a heart that knows true faith. You will be amazed when you do.

Guilt

The emotion of guilt is a tough one. Guilt can exhaust a person's soul. It can rip you apart. It will tear you up from the inside like nothing else. One must beware of guilt. It is because the suffering comes from within. Only you can get rid of the guilt inside of yourself. One must understand that we all make mistakes. We all wish we had done something better. To grow up knowing that we did something wrong can be devastating. We can never go back and fix it. So, we must learn to accept it. We must accept it in our psyche. So that we may make better decisions in the future. We cannot constantly be looking back on our wrongdoings. We must face each day moving forward. Always moving forward. If we are continually looking behind us, we will miss the opportunities we have in front of us.

We all make mistakes. No one is perfect. Do not let those mistakes haunt you. They can only cripple you. You must focus your energy from feeling bad, to feeling good. Happiness is a choice. Motivation is the key to success. You must stay positive to attract the positive. It is Karma. If you want to live a better life, then you must extinguish the guilt within yourself. One cannot carry it around forever. It only has the power to defeat. So many are lost to this truth. A lot of people use guilt as a crutch. They will continue letting their guilt tear themselves apart so that they don't have to feel good about anything. To them, I say, "What a waste of time." Only the self can undo guilt. Strength must be found within. Nothing exterior will expose you to the truth about yourself. What you feel. How hard your life has been. Your goals and aspirations. These are tools for coming clean with your self-guilt. We must live our lives in the light of the day, not in the shadow of it. We must raise our heads high and face the truth. That guilt only has the power to destroy. We must stand up to it. We must walk the path of enlightenment. Shame has no place there. But to get there, we must eclipse the guilt that is inside of us.

Meditation and prayer are excellent tools for battling guilt. They can set us free. Untouched, unblemished by guilt's ugly scar. Just to breathe consciously has the power to fight with the guilt inside of us. So simply live and let the guilt subside from your being. Let it become a distant memory, rather than a future concern. Deal with your guilt head-on and as soon as possible. Do not let it linger into a wound that is hard to heal. Only you have the power to do this. You cannot depend upon anyone else to do it for you. Sharing your guilt is a temporary fix. One must beat it from the inside out. No one else can make your guilt go away.

Do not let guilt make you, its slave. When guilt rears its ugly head, remember, you must find the strength within. The power to tackle your guilt. The strength to live your life free from the despair of guilt. To conquer it within. Once you do this, you can do it a thousand times. A repeatable skill is to battle your existing guilt. It's a method for raising your head high. A path to walk upon in self-worth. This is the truth of guilt and how to defeat it. Upon the path to enlightenment, one will measure oneself. Guilt can only weigh down the spirit. But it cannot defeat it. Remember that guilt is only temporary. The path to the achievable is infinite.

What is greater than a soul without guilt? My answer, "Nothing!" But only you can find the power to defeat it within yourself. Remember that no one is going to do it for you. So, stop searching for truth in others and find it within yourself. You will marvel at its simplicity and be free to move in life according to your own wishes. You will be open to being the person you've always wanted to be, and others will see the strength within you. You can be free of guilt, but you must have the conviction to face it. Once this is done, you can accomplish anything. The door to a larger life will be in front of you. And all you will have to do is merely walk the path. Continue walking, and the truth will become clear. This truth is that the soul cannot be defeated. Unless you allow yourself to be beaten. So, walk through life with your head held high. Be ready to face new obstacles with a newfound certainty. A life of consciousness. A life of progress. And let the world wonder how you did it.

Trust

Trust is an essential emotion. To be able to trust in someone or something can make you feel wonderful. However, to go through life without trust can be a dismal existence. In our lives, in our relationships. We all search for it, and we often do not find it. How nice it is to be able to trust. At the same time, trust can be illusive. We sometimes want it so badly that we fool ourselves into thinking we have it. This can lead to one shying away from a mindset of confidence. This can be harmful. To go through life not trusting anyone will ruin you in the relationships that you have. It will make you feel unwanted. The loneliness you will go through, will never end. Until you decide to let others in and trust once again, you will not know happiness. Happiness is a choice. Believe it.

Trust is something that does not happen right away. You must work for it. It takes time. But once it is acquired, it goes a long way. It is something to live up to. It is something that you do not want to break. Trust, in essence, is what we all want in our lives. However, those who do not find it are miserable. "Once bitten, twice shy." People whose trust has been betrayed will learn to hate the idea of trust. There is nothing worse for a soul then to feel alone. To walk the lonely road. To never experience the happiness of friendship and companionship. Although, to be able to count on someone to always be on your side…is a good thing.

Nothing can be sweeter than to know that you can rely on someone. To be able to depend on someone to be on your side. Through thick and thin. Through the highs and the lows. The ebbs and the floes. Trust is, in some ways, a partnership. A bond. An unbreakable fellowship. Something to be cherished. Something to treasure.

Trust is something we all need to have. How wonderful it is to be able to rely on someone for your own well-being. As well as them being able to rely on yours. Trust is something you must work for. Real trust is not easy. It takes time. It takes effort. One does not just earn trust off the bat. Once it is found though, it is hard to break. It is so valuable to a healthy spirit. It is worth the work to do so. Real trust is priceless. It is impossible to replace. It is something that grows with time.

The basis of every good relationship is trust. Without it your friendships will fail. It is said that "Good things come to those who wait." How true that statement really is. All good relationships take time and effort. Nothing comes easy. So, it is smart to take things step by step. Improving your interactions with others is a piece at a time effort.

This is how you build lasting relationships. You cannot just trust or expect trust immediately. It must be established. Little by little, trust is built. At this point, you must work at it, to keep it. You may ask," What is the point?" I can reply that a lasting relationship is worth it! To be able to depend on others for your welfare is irreplaceable. Something you will value and treasure forever.

So, I say that trust is worth the work. It is worth the time. Worth the effort. A lasting relationship is something that you can have for years. It is something you will treasure for a lifetime. And in the end, you will thank yourself for being a trustworthy spouse, sibling, and friend. Remember, trust is not easy. It takes determination. But it is worth every penny. A lifetime of love and trusting friendship is a bond that is not broken easily. Through all the ups and downs. The ins and outs. The good times and bad.

To depend on someone to be there through all of it… is something precious.

So do not be afraid to put yourself out there. You just might find something extraordinary. Something you thought you would never find. Something you thought could never happen. And the joy you will feel if you give it a chance. The love you will feel in sharing a lasting relationship. I promise it is worth the struggle. It is worth the while. To be able to share with a friend is one of the most powerful forces in life. So, give life a chance. Give love the time to grow. Give joy the room to breathe. Give trust an opportunity. You will be happy that you did.

Anger

Anger is a tricky emotion. Anger can empower one to do great things or do bad things. To learn the balance here is critical. To understand how to use anger is very important. Things can make one angry, life can get the better of you sometimes. Channeling your anger is a powerful force. Anger is a dominant influence in the universe. One must understand how to wield it into something beneficial. Otherwise, it can defeat your consciousness. Positively directing one's energy will guide you on the path you want to be on. The truth of anger is that it is a fire in one's heart. If you let the flame get out of hand, it will dominate your soul's ability to control your actions. Loss of control of your spiritual vigor can be very destructive. It can take you down paths you do not want to go down. It can imprison one's energies and control one's mind. It can harm yourself and others.

Without understanding anger as a spiritual mechanism, it can only lead you upon the wrong track. This can be detrimental to not only yourself but to others. It can empower you to do great and terrible things. It can make you a powerful hero or a terrible villain. To bottle up your anger is the wrong way to deal with it. To channel it positively is the right way to harness it. Meditation, prayer, proper breathing technique, harnessing one's Chi. These are all positive manners of channeling one's anger. Anger is a blaze; if you let it get out of hand, all it will do is consume. You must control your flame. Fire is a dangerous element. Directing its force is the power to do anything. If you can handle the flame of anger, you can master your life.

Many things can cause you to be angry. Difficulties that you face. Hard times, and worse times. You can either handle them or let them consume you. Addressing them will give you the strength you've been looking for. However, if you let anger consume you, all you will have is the power to destroy everything in your path. You must decide what kind of person you want to be in life. Like Shiva, you can be the destroyer or the preserver in life. You must choose a path—the one of destruction or preservation. But you must choose. One will lead you on the way to the achievable, the other to your own personal hell.

All one must do is look in one's heart and determine which type of person you want to be. Your ability to direct your own core is found in the balance between light and dark. The light can illuminate. The darkness can blind you. It is up to you how you want to live your life. Controlling one's anger is the way to do it. Do not let it devour you. Life would just be an open wound to you if you did. The path to the achievable is the insight of one's soul. You must channel your energies to living by this path. The way of, "True North," is the way. For yourself, and everyone around you. You must learn to follow the path. If you want to lead a life of spiritual clarity, being constant is an inexhaustible source of positive energy. Only you can choose to feel it. You can only battle with anger long enough before you learn how to deal with it. You can either continue fighting or accept that it is a natural part of life, and that dealing with it is imperative to your emotional growth.

Do not extinguish the flame, only control it. You do not want to put the fire out. You want to redirect its energies to propel you in a positive state of mind. Directing one's energies to deal with anger has the best results. Put the fire out, and you lose something. Let it burn out of control, and it will engulf. To harness it is the way. The journey is traveled easier with a guiding light. The light of a flame is a candle in the dark—one for all to see. Let your anger be the light. Let others follow it. Let others walk upon the road with you. So that they may shine their lights as well. For all to see. If we all carried our own candles, how wonderful this life would be.

Love

Love is the most powerful and most misunderstood emotion. Love is the balance. It is what keeps us in tune with life. To love is to live, and to live is to love. We search our whole lives to receive love. Only to realize that we must give to receive. We all want things in life. Special things. Things that are meant for us. We can search the globe and never find what we truly are looking for. And love is often found in the strangest of places. You just must know where to look. Love is completion. It cannot be duplicated. It is something new every time. So, we can never have the same thing twice. Many do not understand this fact. It is the "Law of Attraction." People want what they want when they want it. Sadly, this is not love. It is merely wanting. Love is sublime. Because it is new every time. We must experience it every time it comes our way.

People expect to be repaid for their love. People look for love their whole lives and never realize that it is a gift, not a reward. It is reciprocal, but it is something that must be met. Ebb and flow. Wax and wane. Touch and go. Yin and Yang. To love and be loved is the greatest gift one can receive in life. It can be found in anything, and anywhere. The joy we receive in life is the love we give. To someone or something, it does not matter. It all has to do with what we feel about what we love. To love and be loved by someone is truly more excellent. If you feel the worth of the love you give, I can only tell you that you are on the right track.

Love can make you smile. Love can make you frown. My best advice is to feel what you feel when you feel it. Love is like a seesaw. To share in the moments is the gift of love. That is what it is all about. To share in the moments. If you do not, then love is merely wasted. To not be ashamed of what you love. It will only drive you away from the truth.

The truth is, is that love is found in the strangest of places. Sometimes, lightning strikes. To experience it for what it's worth is to be present in the moment. To share with you what you love is what makes life beautiful. It is what makes life worth living. There is nothing you can experience in life that cannot be answered by the ability to understand love. It is all-powerful. It is all-encompassing. You can only understand it by sharing it. It is given before it is yours to receive. So, we try not to take what is given for granted. You never know where love might spring. You never know what is around the corner. Who or what you might feel passion for. That is the beauty and spontaneity of life. Anything can happen at any moment. So, you must keep your eyes open. You never know where life will lead you. It could be just around the corner that you find true love. True love is not a myth. It is the gift of life on Earth. You must give, to share, to understand one another. This is how to love.

So many misinterpret love as something to possess. This sadly is not the case. However, so many are so materialistic as to think that they can own it. So many just want to get a good deal. Give the least and receive the most. Unfortunately, that is not how life works. Life is love held in the balance. The dark and the light. Together to be shared by one another in a constant stream of shared experience. Look out your window and see what life has in store for you. Look to your heart and know what you are willing to give to receive. Only then will you come to grips with the neutrality of love. Something given, something shared. And we meet in the middle, beyond our safety mechanisms. In danger of falling in love with someone, something. To cherish in life is to love forever. So, you must look for this beautiful thing called love. Realize that it is the greatest achievement we can accomplish in life. If you follow love in such a way, if you do not mind being generous with your heart. Then you will undoubtedly find what you have been looking for all along. It may not be today. It may not be tomorrow. But one day you will find the joys of love. Be patient, be forthright, and be generous. And along the way on the path, in the journey we call life, perhaps you will discover the wonders of love. And when you find it, it will be yours to share. Others will see what you have and wonder how you got it. You will shine bright again like the candle that leads the way for others to see. Love is. So don't pay attention to what love isn't. Love is for you. You just must be brave enough to look for it. If you have the courage, then try, try again. One day you will discover it. And it will be everything you thought it would be.

Pain

The emotion of pain is a difficult emotion to bear. Pain is sometimes hard to deal with. However, it occurs when we still suffer from the losses we face in life. It is pain that only goes as far as you let it. Each new pain seems to tear us apart, physically, emotionally, and spiritually. I can tell you that the longer you suffer the pain that you feel, the harder it is to overcome. Years can go by without being able to understand the depths of one's despair.

The decisions we make in life dictate the level of happiness we can feel. The same goes for our mistakes. They can lead us to wonder why we ever made some of the bad choices we have made. We must understand that no one is perfect. We all make mistakes. We all suffer for our bad decisions. However, the way we deal with our shame is up to us. Many doctrines paint a pretty picture of how to deal with one's shame. However, the only path to take is the one you must traverse. No one can do it for you. Every pain is similar. Something like the one before it. You must take each source of pain at its roots. You must undo the knots that tie you up. One knot at a time. One feeling of pain at a time. We must face it with vigor.

We must continue to face our everyday battles and be the best for doing so. To take life head-on and face a new day with positive energy. A positivity that will resonate in your soul. It will stop the agony in one's heart. It will allow you to go through life knowing that there is a brighter side to everything. Without this knowledge, we would linger in grief. Life would seem like a non-stop cycle of misery. Each new day will only compound the pain that you feel.

Nevertheless, it does not have to last forever. You must find it in your heart to forgive yourself for your wrongdoings. You must allow yourself to embrace the pain that you feel. To let yourself feel the pain until it no longer remains. It will warm your heart to the feeling that it is possible to conquer pain. That our choices are made better and more manageable now that we understand our pain.

Pain is illusive. Pain is something that we naturally don't want to feel. Therefore, we are reluctant to do so. To embrace pain means one must lose their fear of it. We must in fact, welcome it. Life is painful. If pain is in the mind, then that is where you must start your journey. Conquering each new source of pain that comes our way. Being willing to deal with the pain is all that is required. The willingness to do so will set you free. With continued practice, you can beat pain as it comes your way. The challenge of dealing with your pain will soon become an instinctive part of your being.

You will no longer walk through life ashamed of your past. The wreckage of your past will soon fade. You will have a new way of looking at life. It will be a positive outlook. Others will see you and wonder how you did it. You will feel free from your physical self, and you will understand how to transcend mere mortality. Your life will take a turn for the spiritual. You will look back upon your worldly being and smile. If the goal in life is to rise above, then you will have accomplished it. How you used to look at life will soon transform. You will no longer look at pain as something to run from, rather than something to be welcomed. Whatever doesn't kill you makes you stronger. If this is true, then dealing with life straight up, no matter what will always be beneficial to you in life. Accepting your fears and emotions into your own hands and dealing with them appropriately. The prolonged effect of not dealing with them is that they will not only remain, but also affect your daily life.

 You want your life to be abundant. Not to be an obligation. Not dealing with the emotion of pain will only become a burden if not faced. Once you learn how to deal with the feeling of pain, a light will go on in your head. You will see what life really is. A series of complicated choices with only two outcomes. Happiness or despair. So, look deep within your soul and choose the life you want to lead. Once you realize the truth, you will see the light. This light can guide you through dark places. This light is the truth. The fact of life is that it is to be enjoyed. But one cannot do so if one does not know the path. The path of, "True North." It is not far. All it takes is a moment of clarity to find it. Once found, it will never leave you. The light will always be there. It will be with you for the rest of your life. And the path to achievement will be at your feet.

So, take care of yourself, your fears, and your emotions. You will be amazed at the outcome. And you will begin to look at life in a better way.

Vice

"Long is the way and hard, that out of Hell leads up to light."

— John Milton

To all things in life, there are always two sides to a coin. The yin and the yang. A light side and a dark side. It is purely natural to experience both. So now let us talk about vice. We all will have some form of vice within us. However, to let it rule, you only can only lead to self-defeat. Upon the path to, "True North," we must find a balance.

Test the waters...so to speak. One cannot suddenly appreciate the light. You must also have a deep understanding of the dark. To obtain this knowledge, you must experience it for yourself. As much as we try to be good people, we all make mistakes. To acquire awareness from these mistakes is the truth. To continue in error is to not learn from those mistakes. As they say, to err is divine, but to continue erring can only lead to downfall. Light will always triumph over the dark. Nevertheless, without the knowledge of the dark side, one can only guess what makes us human. One can be told a thousand times what the right thing is. However, without experiencing it for yourself, denies your humanity.

We all screw up. But to not learn from this will only hold you back. Sometimes we think we're always right. Continuing down the dark path can only lead to your spiritual defeat. To go through life thinking you can only do right is a misinterpretation of the truth. No one is perfect, to try to be perfect is madness. However, once one understands the balance, you learn what it means to be human. It is the space between. Iniquity is natural. Finding a middle way is the path to tread. The uncertainty of life cannot be taught; it can only be experienced. As much as we would like to not make mistakes, it is inevitable. To move forward, we must first learn how to walk. Once we know how to walk, we may run. There is no way to live flawlessly. There are no perfect people, only perfect intentions. However, having impure intentions leads to misunderstanding. This is the path to the dark side. This path also fails you in life. You may spend as much time in error as you want, but eventually, you will have to move on. All there is to do on this path will delay the inevitability of one day having to learn from one's mistakes. As one may enjoy these vices, you will one day understand that they are dead ends. If they are not understood for what they are, then there is no comprehending. Once you have obtained this knowledge, you may realize that they are merely roadblocks. To navigate through vice is to seek understanding. Do not be afraid to fall. Do not be afraid to get back up. Only be afraid of not learning from your mistakes. Life is a journey. Happiness is a choice.

Along the way will be defeats. But there are also victories. Learning and understanding the difference is critical. However, one must experience the truth for oneself. Others will try to build you up. Some will try to break you down. You must make the decision for yourself. How you want to live your life is up to you. Just be aware that there are consequences to your actions. To become comfortable with failing, will only hold you down. To move forward is to understand the truth. The fact is that we all are fallible. We all have faults. We all must get back up and dust ourselves off again. Eventually, we all join back up in the cycle of life. We all begin to move forward again. How long you want to stay stagnant is up to you. When you choose to get back up and move on is also…up to you. Just understand that the direction you want to move in life is forward. However long you want to take to overcome and realize this truth, eventually, we all learn to look at the world this way. Many people feel happy not caring, it comforts them. Some people choose the darkness because all they understand is their imperfections. Some people don't want to feel right about anything. If this is not the path for you, take my advice. Discover the balance. Find "True North." Understand the dark, welcome the light, and propel yourself forward upon the path to the divine. It is not about being perfect. It is about understanding one's imperfections. It is what makes us human. It is what makes you, you. Embrace your failures, but do not accept defeat. Go through life with your head held high. Welcome the future, and smile at the day.

Greed

Avarice, also known as greed, is a powerful force. People are beaten by it. Some are so greedy that they never return from their wreckage. Those that live by greed know no happiness. They will always want more. They will never be happy with what they have. Greed's agenda will consume your humanity. It will devalue all that you have. You will always want more, and because of this, no one will ever be happy. There will be no love higher than the will and want for more. Perhaps it is the perception that with more, one will be satisfied. Are we ever truly satisfied? Maybe, it is how we look at the world around us. We perceive others as having what they want, and we want it too. Who knows what leads to greed, but once you have given into the idea of it, it will engulf your way of life. This is a complicated world to live in. Many looks at greed as a natural part of living. Maybe some just want to fit in. Perhaps they were hurt by the world and want to get back at it.

Success is often confused with personal gain. How does one measure accomplishment? Is it worth the pursuit of happiness or is it the pursuit of having more that drives us. So many are lost in this world to the idea of gain. We are brought up in this world to the understanding that success is the goal. Success is an accomplishment. Happiness is a choice. Benefit is the idea of having more. Often, we compare ourselves to others, and we find that we do not have as much as them. We see others with the things we want to have. We become so lost in the idea of having more that we fail to see the achievement in the things we do accomplish.

Sadly, this is how many live their lives. It is such a prevalent problem that one can distort reality into thinking that greed is a positive value to have. On the contrary, success should not be confused with self-indulgence. It is easy to lose oneself to the idea of having more that we overlook the beauty of simple success. To be happy is to enjoy what we have here on Earth. To want more is the essence of negativity. To put all things aside for personal benefit. To push away others in the quest for more. To let one's soul be consumed with the idea of greed is to lose one's humanity. The one thing that keeps us human is the love for what we have. So, in a way, greed is the quintessence of living a bad life. Even though getting more is the idea that most of us relate to personal success. To not take for granted the value of what one receives as a positive, is the idea of happiness. To be happy with what we obtain is a blessing. To disregard, and disrespect the value of this, is the rapaciousness found in an unhappy soul. It is the heart of greed. It is the devaluation of the gifts we are given.

To be a greedy person is the root of unhappiness. To get what we work for is one thing, but to never be satisfied with what we get is self-defeating. To be thankful for what we genuinely succeed at is positive. The ones we love, the things that we truly value in life. This is the stuff that makes our lives worth living. These are the real successes in our lives. The most beautiful things in life are those successes that truly hold value. To care about materialistic needs is not the path to, "True North." It will devour your soul and leave you empty. To truly live is to give, not to receive. So, we should not fool ourselves with the idea of personal gain. Instead, find ways to give back to the things in life that truly have value: our families, the ones close to us, the ones who need our love. To give and receive from the ones we love is the real success in life. The insanity of greed in this world is overwhelming, and easily confused with success. Do not fall for it. Do not falter into this void. Carry your head high as you move along in this life surrounded by greed. Do not let your heart fall into the abyss of avarice. And you will be well on your way to a happy life.

Laziness

Laziness is a way to forget the real world. Laziness lingers, saps motivation, creates a void between yourself and this planet. It can slowly destroy you. Little by little. Bit by bit. When one wants to forget, we turn away rather than facing our life day by day. Instead, we decide to cherish an absence from the real world. It is almost comforting to ignore what is going on around you. Perhaps we do not want to deal with reality. Maybe we come to realize there is nothing we can do to change it. In this, we find comfort in laziness. We begin to lack the ability to deal with the real world. To exclude oneself is the only grace we can find.

We sometimes believe there is nothing we can do to change the world. The lack of perfection in life can lead those to be consumed by idleness. We find ourselves helpless. Because of this, we choose to withdraw from the world. We choose to hide from the truth and adopt our own beliefs in anguish. Because we choose to be silent, we decide to no longer be a part of everyday life. Choosing laziness is so easy. To run from the truth of reality. Some find solace in not knowing or caring. Over time we decide to forget more of the real world. And we begin to linger in the idea that the world will never change. That there is nothing we can do about it. How terrible life must be for the ones who do not have the strength to live it.

Ignoring the truth about life is a choice. How easy it is to lose oneself, defeat one's very own soul, and crush one's heart. To recede from this world only because one feels they can never change is an endless abyss of forgetfulness. We no longer spend time trying to make the world a better place. Instead, we invest our soul in the negative value of believing that there is no way we can affect the world around us. We must choose to be better, to live better, to make a change. However, the choice is yours. So, it is easy to forget one's role in life. Without the help of others, it is easy to lose faith in life. But to lead by example, you must trust that change is possible. That the more you give, the more you get. The more you hold true, the better you are for it.

 The truth is that it is easy to forget oneself. It is easy to forget one's path. But to stay the course is to be victorious. To be a light in the dark for those who don't believe is the beginning into a world you have not known. To help others find a way is the most rewarding task one can achieve.

And when others see you yearn for life rather than despair, they will praise and follow your example. To humanity, there can be nothing better than to find someone who can be a leader in life. Rather, a failure to face actual reality. The reality is that we all die. But to live a life worth mentioning is a life of progress. Progress in a manner that is incorporated with, "True North." Being aligned with your spiritual compass. If you want to live a healthy life, then disregard the idea of laziness.

Having a lack of interest in life can lead to problems. Problems like depression, and despair. One should always care about where they are in life. With prolonged exposure to apathy, one will lose interest in daily life. It will seem to have no point. Life will have no meaning. Day by day, you will be unable to find happiness or simple delight. You will become stagnant. How can one live life this way? It makes no sense to live a life if you don't see the joy in living. The less interaction you have with your daily life, the more pointless it may seem. To lack a constant spiritual involvement with how you live, will begin to look like the absence of a soul.

Some will turn to other means of happiness. However, these are only temporary fixes. Many will seek addiction as a substitute, such as, addiction to drugs, sex, or guilty pleasure. We will replace a spiritual life with one of obsession. Looking for any new source of satisfaction. Something to fill the void within. The lack of a spiritual life can lead to personal destruction. We replace a life of knowledge with a life of wanted ignorance. This is no way to live life. Think of all that you are missing. Spiritual life will leave one fulfilled every day. A life of indifference can only make one's soul numb. In fact, a life of insignificance will only bring harm to mind, body, and soul. To live like this is tragic. It takes a long time to recover from such a lifestyle. Some are so far gone that they need clinical help. Some may require years of therapy. Only to realize what we need to do, we should have been doing from the beginning. Leading a spiritual life is a conscious effort to live everyday like it mattered. To look for the beauty in life. To look at everyday like it was your last. To make the most of every moment. You will see that even though we will die one day, we can choose to look at life with open arms and open eyes. Whatever mistakes we have made, we forgive ourselves. That we live our lives with a mindful account of our daily lives. To make memories instead of regrets. To take pictures in our minds instead of wanting to forget. To love our lives for what we have been given. To be thankful for every day. To see the beauty in others, instead of with jealous eyes. To focus our energy on a positive direction. To live life to the fullest.

 If you choose to walk down this path, you will not regret it. The spiritual life is the answer to a polluted heart. Even if you have spent years in apathy, if you begin a spiritual quest, you will find what you have been looking for. Finding, "True North," will change your life for the better...every-time. Keeping your soul healthy is as good as any type of medication as you could take. In fact, a healthy soul can heal the body and mind. Many have pondered the extent of the worth of spiritual consciousness. What I may tell you is there is a profit from doing so. The limits are endless. All one must do is look for it. Seek, and you shall find. Find a life of spiritual meaning, and you will never look back. All of this and more can be yours. It all matters how you look at it.

Dishonesty

To be dishonest is wrong. Being dishonest can lead one to think that it is ok to lie and steal. However, just because something is easy does not make it right. To some, the problem is that in our society, getting what you want is more important than being trustworthy. We find that no one cares how you came to possess something. Only that we have it in our possession. The recognition that having stuff is more important than the credit we receive from earning that proprietary. Or so it seems. People driven by material possessions will often lie in the means of obtaining such things. Things we have not worked hard for in the first place. Still thinking that we deserve such things even though we lied to achieve such belongings. This impure act of being deceitful to obtain anything is shunned upon by any good-hearted person. Anyone who lives their lives by the spirit of truth, is successful. The path to achievement is one of honesty. To, "Know Thyself" is one of the only truths we have in life. It is not to be taken lightly.

The spiritual life is one of conscience, it is a way to live without regret. This is far more important than any possession. In life, we will come across things that we would do anything to have. But do not let possession override your willingness to be honest about how you attain such things. To live the path of honesty is to guide yourself upon the path of, "True North." To be honest, is the only way to protect your integrity. Something that never seems to fade. It is always there. All you must do is look at things clearly to see it. So be true. True to yourself. True to others. True to the world you want to be a part of. So, choose honesty. You will be amazed at how much more rewarding it is to be truthful.

Malice

To have malice in your heart is the most destructive vice. To hate is evil. There is no need for it on the journey towards the achievable. Just because someone or something wronged you does not excuse you for having cruelty in your heart. Things don't always work out in life. Sometimes you feel mistreated. Sometimes others do you wrong. Somethings might never go your way. But that does not excuse you from walking a negative path just because you did not get your way. Life may get you down. Life can make you feel like there is no way out. However, to practice forgiveness is a candle in the dark. To let something eat at you is not the way. To forgive is the answer. You will feel better in the end. If you do not get your way, it is not an excuse to be unkind. Holding a grudge will only destroy you. To forgive will purify it. Showing forgiveness to others will make you feel better, but it will make them feel better as well.

Upon the path to, "True North," you will find that to move on one must get beyond one's own hate. To give up on getting one's own way is enlightening. Hating yourself will lead to hating others. Choosing to like yourself and others is the way. You will see that it is the correct path to happiness. In a world filled with hate, be a light in the dark—a candle for all to see. The light of life comes from forgiveness. You will feel better if you do. You will get past all the pettiness of hostility. You will learn the truth of kindness. You will feel the beauty of the soul, and of doing right. It is so simple to practice forgiveness. To hate is the enemy of the soul. It will destroy you.

Jealousy

If you go through life only wanting what others have, then you are living wrong. Jealousy will destroy you. You should be happy with what you have. Wanting something is fine; letting it consume your being is not. You must be thankful for what you have and be glad for others for what they have. To see what others have and dislike them because of it is toxic. You do not want this to control you. You can never find spiritual peace if you look down upon those who possess more than what you hold. Some people have wonderful things; they have beautiful lives. Do not look upon these people with disdain. Be glad that they have what they have. If anything, it will make you want to try harder in life to possess the same. But to be jealous of these same people for what they have just because of what you don't is irrational. One should aspire to be great; we should not be envious of those who have good lives.

What you see on the surface is not always true. Everyone suffers from something. What you see on the exterior is not the whole picture. One must look within for what one truly has. We all have strengths and weaknesses. You may have something that others would like. Would you prefer them to be jealous of you? This is poisonous thinking. We should not want others to be jealous of you the same as you do not wish to be jealous of them. We all must be happy for each other in our successes. Find beauty in our victories. And be there for others when things go wrong. To be jealous of others and to want others to be jealous of us is a sure-fire way to corrupt your being.

We must try to continually move forward. We must try to make our lives here happy ones. To share in this happiness is true bliss. But somehow humanity has gone wrong A humanity where jealousy is the normal. That we should all want to be like a select few. That we are no good, and the only way we can find happiness is to be like everyone else. This is not happiness; it is a prison for your soul. To think that we are no good because we are not like everyone else is absurd. It makes no sense. What do we do when everyone is the same? Perhaps make a world where only the ones who are the same can be beautiful. It's a no-win scenario. You must choose in your soul what type of person you want to be. You must not be afraid to stand out. You can find the beauty within and let it shine to all. Others will see this bright shining light and wonder where it comes from. And if you share it for free, others will thank you for what they receive. Jealousy will not even be an issue. To give happiness to others will reward one's own self. You will see that having a healthy soul is its own reward.

Jealousy over material things will subside. A truth will begin to set in, a truth that has no bounds. To be happy is a state of mind, it's a choice. It's not an article about clothing or a new car. You could throw away all your possessions and still find happiness. You can show others that through you, they can find happiness. Your impact on the world around you will become your source of contentment. Your wanting for material belongings will diminish, and only a profound sense of self will remain. This sense of self will drive you every day. Every waking hour will be an improvement upon yourself. As you improve upon yourself, the ones around you will improve themselves. And this bright shining light will spread until all are content. When no one is jealous, only then can we prosper. So, if you see someone hurting from jealousy, take their hand. If you see someone wanting what they don't have, smile at them. If you have something that someone else needs or wants, give them some of what you possess. Because the only way to keep happiness is to give it away. Let your light shine. Help others to let their light shine. Make the world a brighter place. Leave no one to want, and we will all find solace in what we have. This is the path. Do not be afraid to walk upon it.

Lust

How can one escape desire? How does one overcome the want for pleasure? One can chase it their whole lives and never get enough of it. Sex, power, money, control… All of these can destroy a soul. In moderation, it can be regulated. But when we let it run our lives, it takes over. To try and obtain only pleasure is madness. It will haunt you, there is no escaping it. How does one control the pursuit of it? To want to be happy is one thing; to lust after bliss is foolish. Obviously, we may acquire what we lust after. But is it worth it? Even if we accomplish our goal of achieving something, it can only lead to wanting something else. So how do we control this madness? Changing our goals, perhaps. Fulfilling our wants in moderation, possibly. Maybe it can be as easy as being happy for what we receive. Being humble enough to enjoy the little things in life. To cherish what we have, more than what we do not. All these are possible solutions to the disaster we face when we lust for something. Sex can stain the heart. Control can fool the mind. Power can subdue the soul. If one is to make the journey to, "True North," you must seek reality. If one is to obtain enlightenment. If one is to gain control of the soul's journey. One must understand that some things do not last forever. And those somethings take time. Relationships may fade. Luck may run out. The moment can be lost. But the soul will go on. It all depends on how far you are willing to go. Why waste time on lust when one can enjoy the simple things that we obtain along the way? Why fool oneself into thinking that we can have anything and everything that we want? Simple pleasures, moderation, humility; these all can be the key to battling the depravity of lust. So, choose the path of enlightenment. Choose the road to the achievable. Focus your life's energy on following, "True North." And you can complete your life's quest to a more meaningful existence. The chance to fill the soul with the energy it needs to make the journey. Overcoming lust is a milestone in one's pursuit of happiness. Why believe that we can have whatever we want. Working for something is one thing; chasing unobtainable things is foolishness. Thinking that what we have lasts forever is irrational. All things rise and fall. All things sharp; do dull. What we have one day, we might not have tomorrow. So, love what you have. Cherish what is here today. Do not fool yourself into thinking that you can hold on to things forever. Let go of the things you fear to lose, and you will overcome. Realize that all things are here one day and gone the next, and you will succeed in life. Fear will subside, and you will open the door to a larger existence. Choose wisely, and you can accomplish your goals. But remain humble, for all things fade away.

Pride

Finally, we come to pride. Hubris can be very dangerous. It is good to feel a sense of accomplishment. Accomplishment is a good thing. To be driven only by achievement can damage the soul. Thinking that you are better than others can damage relationships. Holding yourself above, others can only bring you, and those around you harm. Ego can harm as much as anything can. Some people drive themselves mad, trying to attain their whole lives. Life is more than achievement. To rise above, does not mean that you are better than others. You can fool yourself for a lifetime in thinking this. To rise above means to put petty things away and accept a higher state of being. Success in your soul is so much more important than success in a purely self-centered manner. To help others rise above is so much more fulfilling than success in a narcissistic way. To want others to see your accomplishments is self-centered. To help others succeed is more rewarding on so many levels. To want only for yourself is greedy. To want more than others is wrong. You may work hard for a lifetime. And the fruits of your labors are rewarding. To take away from others' success, only to service your own personal sense of pride is inappropriate. Everyone deserves a piece of the pie. Not in a material sense. But in a spiritual one. All you must do is be courageous enough to see that everyone can be as good as anyone else. They just need to be pushed to their own limits, and sometimes, beyond. When one is pushed to their limits, you can see their greatness. Success should be in the journey and not the destination. Pride can fool you into thinking you are better than others. It is essential to let go of yourself, if you truly hope to rise above. To rise above one's personal limitations is healthy. To assume that you are already virtuous is only going to harm you.

To drive others to greatness is a reward in and of itself. To see other's moments of triumph can be so much more rewarding than personal achievement. To want to show off your accomplishments is selfish. Selfishness leads to destruction. Destruction leads to loss. It is better to know one's strengths and keep them, rather than show them off. It only hurts others when you boast.

On the other hand, to help others achieve is the fruit of life. To show others the light is most rewarding. When one recognizes their own accomplishments for what they are worth, is its own achievement. So much more than personal endeavors. Accomplishing for others can make you feel a healthy sense of pride. But when pride is fueled only for personal reasons, it can deceive you onto a path of personal defeat. Don't get me wrong, a healthy sense of pride can be rewarding, even helpful in some ways. But to let it drive your life will take away from the beauty of sharing life with others. If helping others is your goal, then setting specific personal objectives to accomplishment is good. But when one wants only for self, it will leave you wanting for more.

Too much of a good thing can be harmful. To only be driven by personal success can trick the mind into thinking that you are better than you really are. To meet this head-on and accomplish certain things is good. But to boast and brag of one's own personal feats can harm the esteem of others. It will set unnatural limitations upon oneself. To strive for perfection is one thing. To think you are perfect is and always will be false. This is how pride can destroy. No one is perfect—only perfect intentions. And we should use those intentions to fuel healthy relationships with others that are not based upon personal accomplishment. To compete is healthy. To assume that you are better than others is deceptive. To meet yourself and others head-on and take the challenge of life for what it really is can be a great release from one's own personal struggles.

To understand one's limitations and to stretch yourself to the task of meeting those goals is how pride should really work. However, most do not understand this. We are only as great as we make ourselves to be. And others are only as great as we allow them to be. We must work together in a common goal to all find success. To cherish these moments of victory is what makes us have genuine pride. Not driven off self, but off shared compassion amongst others. So, choose proper fulfillment, and do not fool yourself into thinking you are better than others. We all deserve a chance to shine. And to let others shine will bring you real pride. So, choose wisely.

Virtue

"The happiness of your life depends upon the quality of your thoughts."

-Marcus Aurelius

Virtue is the good that we make of ourselves, and the good we see in others. We live in it every day. We face it every morning when we wake up, and when we go to sleep at night. It is merely the decisions we make every day to be better people. It can be difficult sometimes because life will knock us down. However, we have the choice to get back up. Virtue is what we hold on to. It is in us and those around us. We see it when we look out the window. We feel it when we open doors for others. We all aspire to something greater than ourselves. This is a virtue.

Virtue is the understanding that there are things in life that are evil; that we can steer ourselves upon the righteous path to better living. We see someone hurting and want to help them. We see someone doing something wrong and reach out to them. We see those who struggle and lend a hand. Once we appreciate that we can make a difference, not only in our lives but also in others' lives. Then we are set free. To know that we can make a change, to make this world a better place. This is the real achievement we are all searching for. To live virtuously every day. To share our virtue with others to make them better. To know that what we do every day makes a difference within ourselves. It soon becomes a pattern, and we find a life of virtue is a life worth living.

Beyond all the wicked ways of some, we strive to be better people. And in that, we are better people. People will see us and find that living a good life is based upon the choices we make. Then they, too, will make the right choices. To understand that the choices we make determine all the difference in our lives and the lives of those around us. This is an understanding of a life of virtue. It can be called a moral decision. To make the choice to be better people every day of our lives is the path to real happiness, and contentment. We find the power to do this through virtue. It reaches far beyond all the wickedness in the world. Like a bright shining light, a torch in the darkness. Like the light of a new day. Something to guide us all into a better existence. To lead ourselves and those in need, is to have virtue. When we alter ourselves into a virtuous life, others will see it and want it too. This will change the world around us. Little by little, bit by bit. If you believe in this, then you believe in truth, you believe in virtue. If you believe in virtue, you can accomplish anything. To change ourselves and those around us is a noble path. Something we should all strive for in life. This noble path is before our feet. All we must do is walk it. Walk the path, and others will follow. This is one of the most important things you may accomplish in life. To spread love and virtue to the world around you. This is the path to, "True North," which is the path to virtue. All life feeds off the positive energy that we convey through ourselves. So, live the good life, walk the noble path... choose virtue.

Patience

Patience is key. Patience in all things. We must be patient with what we want in life. We must be patient when obtaining our goals. We must understand that we don't just automatically get what we want along the way. That anything good, takes work. To take things one step at a time. Patience is good. It helps us value what we obtain in this life. When we set our sights on an objective, we must be patient in the ways in which we pursue that objective. It is important to take our time with these pursuits. So that we know the real value of all things we get in this existence. Patience is not easy. We often want to get what we want, when we want it. However, we must be strict with our wants and desires. We do not just automatically get to have whatever we want in life. Everything we get in life must be worked for, or it has no true value. This is a good thing. It teaches us to work hard for the things we want in life. A good work ethic teaches us that patience is an advantage in acquiring one's goals and ambitions. Trying to look at life with patient eyes teaches us to remain calm. To see things through. That no matter what life throws at us, we will be vigilant in the pursuits of that which we wish to achieve.

We see at this time in our lives that all around us, people just want to get what they want when they want it. Perhaps we are jealous of this. Do not be led astray. Immediate gratification is an illusion. Nothing good comes from getting what we want without having found the virtues in what it takes to achieve it. That in toiling to achieve our goals we find the very heart of understanding. Understanding the purpose behind our own good fortune is to know the value of what we have accomplished. Patience is on the road to contentment. On this road you will struggle. For contentment is the goal. Patience is the first step to getting there. So always be aware of what it takes to achieve our goals and be patient for the world to come.

Courage

Courage moves you forward. Courage makes you strong. It is the driving force to continue life's journey. We all have times in our lives when we get knocked down. Having courage will help you get back up. The courage to endure what life will throw at you is truly remarkable. This virtue will help guide you upon your path. The courage to look inside and see what one truly has is helpful in so many ways. To face not only our weaknesses but to find our strengths. When we see ourselves how we are, we gain the ability to recognize our actual character. To focus our energy on trying to make ourselves better is courage in and of itself. Often, we find ourselves in dark places. Life can hold us down. We will all face difficulty in our lives. But to endure and face adversity shows who we truly can be. It not only gives us strength, but it gives others the courage to face themselves as well. I know that it can be daunting, but to lose courage in one's heart is to give up on life. We cannot give up on ourselves. We cannot give up on life. It is all part of the journey. To understand where we are in our hearts and in our minds is to find that courage within ourselves. The courage to go further, the courage to rise above. To hold our heads high. To give others the courage to do the same. It is what we live for every day. To see courage in others inspires us to see the courage within ourselves. It is the drive that sends us onward. That moves us past the hardships that we face. The light that shines in the dark. The light for all to see. The needle on the compass. Do not be afraid to let the light within shine. Others will look up to you. It will guide them forward. Until all that we have is the drive to move on. This is the power of courage. Do not be frightened, it is only yourself that you must gain.

Wisdom

Wisdom is an important steppingstone in knowing and applying virtue. It is what we seek. It is what we want to know about. It wants us to know. Knowledge is power. A wise man is richer than a king. A wise man knows the truth. Wisdom is better than jewels. Truth is what we all pursue. Wisdom is freedom. Understanding will make a soul complete. Our souls long for the truth. In wisdom, we will look at reality through constant eyes. Knowledge is what is learned. Wisdom is what is gained. Wisdom guides us. We can search our whole lives, and we can never be wise enough.

An unwise man thinks he knows everything. However, a wise man is a man who realizes that what he knows is little. Arrogance is wisdom's enemy. Someone who does not know can always learn. One who thinks he knows everything can learn little. In life, we are always learning. Always striving for more. Those who seek possessions are foolish. Those who seek knowledge are brilliant. The more we learn, the more we grow. To grow like a plant. To realize that the world is too big to know everything is at the heart of wisdom. Wisdom comforts. It makes us feel upright. It helps us through life. It allows us to recognize the difference between fiction and fact. We see each other more clearly with wise eyes. We are no longer easily fooled. The little things in life begin to amuse us. Wisdom comforts. It brings calm to the soul. How does one become wise? Simple. One seeks but cannot find something so basic as a good lesson. We must breathe and see the truth. That the human condition is real. We cannot escape our existence. So instead of fighting it, embrace it. See that we are only mortal. That any day may be our last. Life is more beautiful from this point of view. It is more tangible. Some may worry because of this reality. Do not be troubled.

The truth is, is that we are all dying. Life in every breath is the only way to live. Once we understand this, we can look at life for what it is. It is a brief moment that we find ourselves. We must always look for these moments, and not run from them. We must cherish them. We must embrace the fact that we live short lives. But with this knowledge brings a recognition of the truth. We begin to see the moment. We begin to overcome our fears. We start to see life with pure emotions. With this knowledge, we begin to live in the moment. We overcome our weaknesses and begin to find strength. We become wise. We grow in our age and contemplate beauty. And life is always right in and of itself. This is the noble path. This is the path to happiness. This is wisdom.

Integrity

To speak the truth is the very essence of virtue. To be true. To be honest. To be whole. To be one. One must embrace their inner self. One must seek it with their heart. To be able to say that I will embrace honesty is a truly wonderful thing. To know that in one's soul, "I am true," is the most basic reality that anyone can hold. To know thyself is to have integrity. Truth surrounds and binds us. Keeps us real. Keeps us honest. There is no fooling someone with integrity. However, some would seek to take advantage of someone who has integrity. Yet it can never truly harm us because we know ourselves. One who has integrity can stand tall. It is a shield that protects us. Those who know themselves can never be left in ruin. We know that whatever happens, at least we have our integrity. At least we have our truth. It will boggle the mind what some people go through to gain. But for one with integrity, the truth can never hurt us. For we are trustworthy. We know our hearts. We understand our minds. We believe in something that can never diminish. We believe that we must always speak the truth, even if it means we suffer for it. In this manner, we can never truly be conquered.

The golden rule will never decline in its value. To treat others as we want to be treated. It is as good today as it ever was. Those who live by it will know themselves to be true. This has value to anyone who seeks it. Those who seek an honest manner will know a truthful life. It will never falter. The benefit of honesty is knowing that we get exactly what were worth. No more, no less. To live life in such a manner is comforting to one's soul. We sleep better at night. And every night we go to bed and smile for that day. Only to wake up and do it all again. The truth is comforting. To know we know ourselves is a relief. To keep one's soul intact, every day, is a blessing. To expect no less from the act of being. To demand no less from others. To live life in such a fashion is immensely gratifying. It is something we can confide in. To understand when we are wrong. This is the basis of integrity. To admit one's wrongs is to set one's soul free. Like a bird on a wing. To always keep ourselves in balance. This is to have integrity. For those who believe in themselves, is stronger than any force on Earth. It has no substitution.

There is no replacement for honesty. For those who live their lives in such a way, can only know comfort. For our well-being is strong. Nothing can penetrate it. Integrity is impervious to anything. It is a castle that knows no conqueror. It is a journey that has no end. It is constant, like the seasons. Something we can count on. Something dependable. Something that soothes those who know it. To have integrity is to be true. To be true is all anyone can ask of us. It is all we can ask from others. To be honest, is to know this. To be grateful for ourselves is what makes us human.

Humility

Humility is at the very heart of virtue. One cannot be virtuous without knowing humility. One must look at the world through appropriate eyes. To be calm, to be simple, this is the breadth of virtue. The world has many distractions. However, the calmness of the mind is the only way to see the world. To be understanding of one's own situation in life is the path to freedom. To see life with open eyes. To live is to appreciate one's own situation. Life may hold us down; we must always be able to hold ourselves up. No matter what happens to us, we must be grateful for what we receive. To dream of a better life is one thing. To live in quiet contemplation and recognize one's own direction in life is valuable. One cannot advance in life until they understand where they come from. We all start small. But if one humbly looks at life, one can accomplish their goals. It may move slowly at first, but with continuous effort, one can achieve one's goals in life. To fool oneself into thinking, they are better than what they are is deceptive. Looking at the sky is a good thing. To keep one's feet on the ground, however, is more important. Dreams and ambitions are healthy. Nevertheless, being humble and grateful for what one receives is the most essential lesson life can offer. To be appreciative and glad for what one attains is true happiness. To be humble and happy is a choice.

Life can be confusing when always looking to the next big thing. But to accept what one obtains in the struggle of life is the path to contentment. With the knowledge of humility, to be grateful, to be unwavering, is the road to success. Taking life, a day at a time. To be thankful for what one receives. One who has this knowledge is their own master. To be master of the self is truly the most significant accomplishment one may acquire in life. Every little thing one receives in life is something to be thankful for. One may want to conquer a mountain, but unless you are willing to climb it, it is difficult. For one who is ready to put one foot in front of the other and ascend, it is merely an obstacle in one's way. One day at a time, one step at a time is the path to real success. In mind, in body, and in soul. Those who are humble can accomplish anything. Without the understanding of modesty, one will never truly see what one has in life. Just taking a moment out of every day to sit in quiet contemplation is enough to appreciate one's situation. To embrace one's condition will give you wings. To try to fly high above one's difficulties is good. However, one must eventually land. To know where one stands is genuinely something to appreciate. Humility will help you keep your goals and ambitions in check. You will understand your place in life. You will be grateful for what you receive. No one could ask for more in life than to look at life through soft eyes. To see things for what they truly are. This is the power of humility.

Strength

Strength is the monument built by the stone of virtue. The more we practice virtue, the stronger we become. The more we experience life in the right way, the stronger we are. We all wonder if we are strong enough. The only way to determine this is by living life correctly. Every step we take in the right direction makes us stronger. Some people are afraid of their own strength. For whatever reason, some are fearful of their own personal resilience. The ability to lead oneself and to lead others must be recognized directly. Learning how to use one's strength is beneficial. Running away from the obligation that one must control one's life is to cheat themselves. There will not always be someone there to guide you. At some point in one's life, one must step up to the plate and swing. Only through right action does one find strength. It all comes down to what you do with it every day, to be a good person...or not. Those who stand with strength are unbeatable. One must lead themselves upon this route. There will not always be someone there to tell you what to do. In these moments, we find our true strength. We find it when we take control of our lives. We see it in helping others. We find it by reflecting upon our own actions. As well as the actions of others. For some, strength is a burden. For those who do not want to lead. For those who want the occupation of guiding others, strength is an ally. People will look up to you. They will take your advice. They will act rightly within the blanket of your leadership. Those who are guided by strength come to see strength in themselves. They may also wake up one day and decide to lead. If you dare to wake up and realize that you must break ground sometimes and be in charge, then you will find in your heart that you are strong. Find your inner strength.

Follow your, "True North." Take your place along with all those who have the strength to lead. I guarantee you will like what you find when you look at yourself and see the strength within your very being. You can trust it in your heart. You will discover the right action, and your mind will know itself. To understand what you are truly made of. Find strength and fight for what is right. Not only for yourself. But for those who have not yet found the strength within themselves. Be the rock that builds the monument. And last forever with the strength to do the right thing every day of your life.

Compassion

Compassion is a vital virtue. A compassionate heart can heal any wound. Kindness is the ultimate truth. To do what is right for yourself and others. Sometimes doing the right thing makes no sense. But if you follow the path of compassion, you will understand why it is crucial to living a virtuous life. What is most beneficial... How do we determine that? How do we know that what we are doing is the right thing? To follow your heart and to do what you feel is the right thing is sometimes hard to see. Others may disagree with you along the way. But you must choose to follow your heart and trust in right action. Compassion is the goal of all virtue. To be kind. To love your neighbor. To do right by yourself and others. To live life with love. To forgive. To be caring for all living things. To know in your heart and soul that what you do is beneficial to all. To live life generously. To do a favor and expect nothing in return. A wise man once said, "A kind word is better than charity followed by insult." To look at the world through kind eyes. To help those in need. To be charitable. To love life and all things. To do for others as you would do for yourself. This is compassion. This is what is most beneficial. To live in the right action. To have the right thoughts. If you live your life in this manner, you will be amazed at how wonderful life can be. You will look upon yourself and others and smile. You will know true happiness. You will share with others and spread love to those around you. Others will look upon you as a pillar of virtue. They will look up to you, and they, in turn, will do the same for others. You will find value in small things, and you will see how simple being compassionate is. You must see with open arms and eyes. It will change the way you look at the world.

Others will see you and want what you have. Compassion grows like a plant. It spreads as far and wide as it can seem to grow. Life goes on. To find solace in that fact is a good beginning. To feel life in the moment. To experience the human condition with open eyes is to see life for what it is. Once you look upon life in such a matter, you can begin to see what doing the right thing can accomplish. If you keep looking at life in such a matter, compassion becomes a habit. The habit becomes a custom. Custom changes your life. And you will see who you really are. Compassion has the power to change lives. So, change yourself, and you will see how it transforms those yourself and those around you.

Honor

Honor is the zenith of all virtue. Only found when all other virtues are embodied. It is the culmination of all your ventures in life. To be true to thy self in a manner that respects all, is to have honor. To treat others as you want to be treated. To expect perfection in oneself. To look for the ultimate quality in life. To always be aware of what is most beneficial. This is to have honor. The path to honor is found in the excellence of the mind, the heart's passion, and the discipline of the soul. It is the pinnacle of self. Its virtue can only be found in the calm awareness of the mind. A manner of living that reflects one's values of life. The understanding of the human condition and the importance of existence. This is the root of honor. Honor is eternal; it is the accumulation of all virtue. To find honor in oneself is to understand life. To hold in esteem all things found in life. To look at the world as a whole and live by all virtues, is to live life by the code of honor. A principle that is simple. To find the discipline to live by this code will instill upon one the knowledge of being. The truth that lies within...

Life in every breath.

To look at the world through perfect eyes. To see in all a faultless manner. To transcend the corporal world and enter one without fault. To live by an eternal code of perfection. To demand in oneself the embodiment of virtue. To respect all living things, and to do right by them. This is how to live a life of honor. The values of all things become a sacred path for the soul. A venture everyone must take eventually. When we leave this world, we must understand the concept of honor. Because it is the perfection of self. It is the heart of virtue and the root of being. The source of all goodness, the end of the means, is personified in everything we do. To understand this is to have honor. The truth to all worldly endeavors is to see them for what they are. To live by honor is to see the world in such a way. To walk this path will guide you to the height of all existence. The path is before your feet. You must choose to walk the path eventually. So, to begin with the understanding of life is to be born. Born of honor. Born of virtue.

Finally on Dry Land

"Carefully watch your thoughts, for they become your words. Manage and watch your words, for they will become your actions. Consider and judge your actions, for they have become your habits. Acknowledge and watch your habits, for they shall become your values. Understand and embrace your values, for they become your destiny."

-Mahatma Gandhi

To be content is the most sublime experience in life. To be happy for what you have is more powerful than any want. To want is vanity. To love and cherish, what you've been given is a thousand prayers. We all hope for wonderful things; we all want a beautiful life. But to continue to want for what one does not have can be harmful. To be greedy in life is a lowly existence. To treasure those we love, and the moments we have with each other is the greatest gift we have in life. Life is full of hardships; there are many obstacles to overcome. But to go the distance for those we care for is the most rewarding of all desires. To experience life and all its challenges, overcome difficulties, and rise above our life's trials. These are all beautiful things. Wisdom is better than jewels.

All the anger, love and pain in life is what makes life worth living. A good life is one set by strength, compassion, and honor. In and among itself, contentment is such a beautiful place to be. To understand the importance of being calm, of relaxation. A present mind, and a peaceful heart, will lead to a happy soul. To share what we have with those closest to us is the greatest gift we can receive. Even without possessions, one can value the simple things in life. To recognize the importance of a tranquil mind is a wonderful feeling. To find a quiet understanding of life's lessons. The world can be a beautiful place. A peaceful existence can be the most rewarding accomplishment we can achieve. Some strive for perfection and never reach it. Some chase a life of possession. For some they can never have enough. For a spiritual life, these things cannot bring joy. The only true joy is being ourselves, the experiences we treasure, and being with the ones we love. Happiness is the moment…Happiness is a choice. If we stray from a spiritual existence, then we may never find true happiness. Life is short, we must learn to value the simple things.

To find real pleasure, one must not stray from the truth. The truth is simple. Contentment comes from a peaceful presence of mind. It comes from a giving heart. It finds itself in our souls. It leads us down paths that we want to go down. Roads paved with gold will no longer have the same luster. We will want for nothing and appreciate what we have. Here and now is our presence of mind. The future and the past will slip away. We will no longer want what we do not have. We will learn to appreciate the value of life. We will find true contentment and be the best for it. Choose the right path. Find your real happiness. Live your life like it was your last day. You will be well for it. You will understand life in a whole new way. Share it with others and find true contentment, live experience with open hands, hearts, and minds. Be better for it.

So now you see now that everything is a part of a larger picture. All of it is part of the same equation. The human condition. We are all human, and yet, we are all different...and the same. That we are exactly where we should always be in the universe. What we seek and desire is how we find ourselves in life. Experiencing life in all its forms. That we understand where we come from, so we know where we are going. All the trials we face in life. All the understandings we come to find. We are all part of the same bigger picture. All our fears, emotions, all our vices and virtues. From the elements of the earth to our own animal instincts. All the pitfalls we face in life that keep us going down the wrong path. From all our ideas to all our philosophies. All our understandings and all the intangibles that we come to appreciate along the way. The ability to guide our way through life. All the beginnings and all our destinations. We live in it every day, whether we know it or not. All of us face the same difficulties. Life is geometric. Our everyday lives are lived in the same design. We all share the same life experience, just under different conditions. The situation may change, but the understanding is the same. We live, we grow, and we realize the truth. That we are all part of the same plan. The human condition is meant to be lived. Whether you know what you are doing or not. We are all part of it. In this book, all I have done is put the pieces together. So, you can come to realize the truth. It is a simplification of many beliefs. All of them somehow someway mean the same thing. This pattern, this way, this life. Once you come to realize the truth. Once you comprehend the reality of it all. Once you can locate yourself at any given moment in life. Then you have come to face life in all its simplicity. To search for the achievable. To live by your spiritual and moral compass. To follow "True North" is to comprehend life, in all its ambiguity. To know when you are lost. To know how to guide your way. To not stress over the little things. To appreciate life for all its twists and turns. To recognize that there are good times, and there are bad times. To live life through all of life's tribulations. To know thyself. To be willing to take on what life has to offer. To neither run away nor hide from reality. To not fool yourself in difficult situations. To take life head-on and grab it by the horns. To understand that there is a purpose to all of it. That life can knock you down. That you must get back up. That you must drive on. Through the good and the bad. This book merely simplifies these truths. I wrote it to help you understand that once you have come to realize these truths, there is nothing you can't accomplish. Follow your compass. Follow, "True North."

I wrote this book to signify the moments where we lose and find ourselves. A spiritual and moral compass is merely a tool you can use to navigate through life better. Through all its difficulties and misfortunes. Through all its pinnacles and all its trenches. All you have to do is understand life in its simplicity. To learn how to read the compass. To know where you are at any given point in your life. Once realized, you can achieve anything. Find your, "True North." Live spiritually, realistically, and most importantly, live completely. Once you have sharpened yourself to this point, life will become easy. You will understand things that used to baffle you. You will find out how to get back up when knocked down. You will cherish the good. Learn from the bad. And carry on.

Most importantly, you will understand what it means to live. And that is all you must do in life. How you live your life and how you respond to things is the only thing that you have control over. Remember, you are exactly where you need to be in the universe. Embrace that principle. Pass on that understanding. It is easy to pass the knowledge to others. In doing so you will gain the power of life through what you pass on. To light a candle for others. So, hold onto the light, and pass it on to all the ones around you. To give away knowledge is the only real power we have. Live for it all, don't waste a second. Live right up to the hilt. Forget the past, embrace the present, look forward to the future. And live. What have you got to lose? Thank you. Let your spirit stay on the path to, "True North."

www.ingramcontent.com/pod-product-compliance
Lightning Source LLC
Chambersburg PA
CBHW081123300726
48977CB00004B/869